SAPPHO'S JOURNAL

BOOKS BY
PAUL ALEXANDER BARTLETT

NOVELS

VOICES FROM THE PAST:
Sappho's Journal • *Christ's Journal* • *Leonardo da Vinci's Journal*
Shakespeare's Journal • *Lincoln's Journal*

When the Owl Cries

Adiós Mi México

Forward, Children!

POETRY

Wherehill

Spokes for Memory

NONFICTION

The Haciendas of Mexico: An Artist's Record

SAPPHO'S JOURNAL

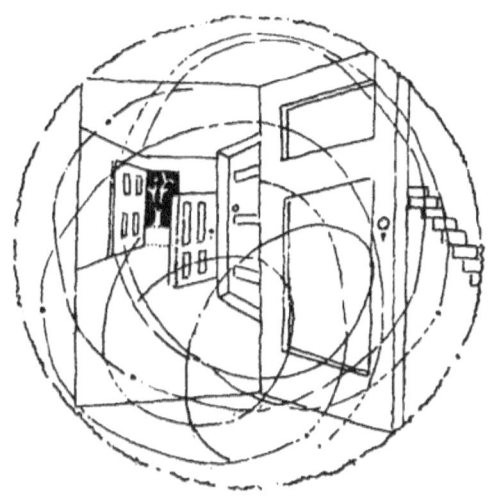

by
PAUL ALEXANDER BARTLETT
and
Illustrated by the Author

Edited by
STEVEN JAMES BARTLETT

with a FOREWORD by
WILLIS BARNSTONE

"Violet-haired, pure
honey-smiling Sappho"
– Alcaeus

AUTOGRAPH EDITIONS
Salem, Oregon

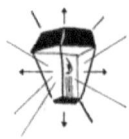

AUTOGRAPH EDITIONS
P. O. Box 6141 • Salem, Oregon 97304

ℛ Established 1975 ℘

Copyright © 2007 by Steven James Bartlett
First Edition

ISBN 978-0-6151-5646-0

Library of Congress Catalog Card Number: 2006025662

Printed in the United States of America

Library of Congress Cataloguing-in-Publication Data

Bartlett, Paul Alexander.
  Sappho's journal / by Paul Alexander Bartlett and illustrated by the author ;
edited by Steven James Bartlett ; with a foreword by Willis Barnstone. -- 1st ed.
    p. cm.
  Summary: "A historical novel that recounts the life, thought, and times of the
Greek poet Sappho of Lesbos, based on a study of ancient Greece and
Sappho's surviving fragments of poetry"--Provided by publisher.
  ISBN 978-0-6151-5646-0
  1. Sappho--Fiction. I. Bartlett, Steven J. II. Title.

PS3602.A8396S27 2006
813'.6--dc22

                                                          2006025662

CONTENTS

FOREWORD

Willis Barnstone

Distinguished Professor Emeritus of Comparative Literature
Indiana University

*P*aul Alexander Bartlett's journal of Sappho is a masterful work. I had recently completed a translation of the extant lines of Sappho and am familiar with his problems. He was faced with the almost impossible task of reconstructing the personality of Sappho and her background in ancient Lesbos. To my happy surprise he did so, in a work which is at once poetic, dramatic and powerful. In *Sappho's Journal* he does more than create a vague illusion of the past. He conveys the character of real people, their interior life and outer world. A mature artist, he writes with ease and taste.

PREFACE

Steven James Bartlett

Senior Research Professor of Philosophy, Oregon State University
and
Visiting Scholar in Psychology & Philosophy, Willamette University

*S*appho's Journal is one of five independent works of fiction which together make up *Voices from the Past*, a quintet of novels that describe the inner lives of five extraordinary people. Progressing through time from the most distant to the most recent they are: Sappho of Lesbos, the famous Greek poet; Jesus; Leonardo da Vinci; Shakespeare; and Abraham Lincoln. For the most part, little is known about the inward realities of these people, about their personal thoughts, reflections, and the quality and nature of their feelings. For this reason they have become no more than voices from the past: The contributions they have left us remain, but little remains of each person, of his or her personality, of the loves, fears, pleasures, hatreds, beliefs, and thoughts each had.

Voices from the Past was written by Paul Alexander Bartlett over a period of several decades. After his death in an automobile accident in 1990, the manuscripts of the five novels were discovered among his as yet unpublished papers. He had been at work adding the finishing touches to the manuscripts. Now, more than a decade and a half after his death, the publication of *Voices from the Past* is overdue.

Bartlett is known for his fiction, including *When the Owl Cries* and *Adiós Mi México*, historical novels set during the Mexican Revolution of 1910 and descriptive of hacienda life, *Forward, Children!*, a powerful antiwar novel, and numerous short stories. He was also the author of books of poetry, including *Spokes for Memory* and *Wherehill*, the nonfiction work, *The Haciendas of Mexico: An Artist's Record*, the first extensive artistic and photographic study of haciendas throughout Mexico, and numerous articles about the Mexican haciendas. Bartlett was also an artist whose paintings, illustrations, and drawings have been exhibited in more than 40 one-man shows in leading museums in the U.S. and Mexico.

Archives of his work and literary correspondence have now been established at the American Heritage Center of the University of Wyoming, the Nettie Lee Benson Latin American Collection of the University of Texas, and the Rare Books Collection of the University of California, Los Angeles.

Paul Alexander Bartlett's life was lived with a single value always central: a sustained dedication to beauty, which he believed was the most vital value of living and his reason for his life as a writer and an artist. *Voices from the Past* reflects this commitment, for he believed that these five voices, in their different ways, express a passion for life, for the creative spirit, and ultimately for beauty in a variety of its forms—poetic and natural (Sappho), spiritual (Jesus), scientific and artistic (da Vinci), literary (Shakespeare), and humanitarian (Lincoln). In this work, he has sought, as faithfully as possible, to relay across time a renewed lyrical meaning of these remarkable individuals, lending them his own voice, with a mood, simplicity, depth of feeling, and love of beauty that were his, and, he believed, also theirs.

The journal form has been used only rarely in works of fiction. Bartlett believed that as a form of literature the journal offers the most effective way to bring back to life the life-worlds of significant, unique, highly individual, and important creators. In each of the novels that make up *Voices from the Past,* his interest is to portray the inner experience of exceptional and special people, about whom there is scant knowledge on this level. During the many years of research he devoted to a study of the lives and thoughts of Sappho, Jesus, Leonardo, Shakespeare, and Lincoln, he sought to base the journals on what is known and what can be surmised about the person behind each voice, and he wove into each journal passages from their writings and the substance of the testimony of others. Yet the five novels are fiction: They re-express in an author's creation lives now buried by the passage of centuries.

I am deeply grateful to my wife, Karen Bartlett, for her faithful, patient, and perceptive help with this long project.

✧

For my father,
Paul Alexander Bartlett,
whose kindness, love of beauty and of place
will always be greatly missed.

Sappho's poetry, quoted throughout this novel, is included with the translator's permission. The poems appeared in *Sappho, Lyrics in the Original Greek*, with translations by Willis Barnstone, Anchor Books, Doubleday, 1965.

For clarity, the calendar used by Sappho has been translated into our modern calendar.

Sappho's Journal

Sappho, walking on her island beach,
pauses by a broken amphora:
With one foot, she nudges the terra cotta and black jar,
its painted chariot, charioteer and horses:
The charioteer wears a laurel wreath.
Sappho, about 30 years old,
her hair braided around her head,
naked, sandaled, saunters along the Mediterranean,
gulls and pelicans flying, surf and gull sounds in early morning yellow.

*T*he great storm beats across the island, rattling the olive and the cypress, piling the surf on the beach, hissing the rain across my roof. It is cold and the light of my terra cotta lamp is cold. Some say that a storm will wash away our island, but I do not believe it. Our island will be here long after I have gone, and so will our town, my dear Mytilene, so wrong, so right.

Alcaeus would revel in this gale and go out in it and let the rain lash him and then he would come and take me in his arms.

The storm will rage all night and the gutters spew, and I will rage at my solitude, a solitude that grows and grows.

Growl on, spew on, beat and tramp—tomorrow's sun will return and the sea's eye will glitter and I will gaze across the bay—and Alcaeus will not be here.

My feet are cold and the lamp is weak and the wax hard, and I must go to bed.

Yesterday, the wine workers gathered at a nearby vineyard, old men and girls, in tattered clothes, some lazy, some hard-working, pressing the grapes, many of them my friends. Spade-bearded Niko directed the pressing, sitting at the base of an oak, wearing a stained robe, his voice low. Women carried hampers of grapes loaded with purple clusters, the women's skirts wet with dew, the grapes mottled with damp. Clouds made the day cool. Someone toyed with a flute, the men treading, emptying husks over sandy soil, now and then pausing to talk under the oak, the circular press letting out its red, everyone tasting. Many amphorae were broken, before they were finally filled and capped.

I wanted to help. How sweet the smell flooding my nose.

Atthis has been my girl-child today and we have strolled together up the long, long path to the outcrop, beyond the temple. Atthis and tall white marble columns, with their busy apricot-breasted swallows, have assuaged my loneliness. How lonely we become, as we grow older, even when there is someone to share. The key to self gets lost; self-assurance diminishes. Once, it was only necessary to dash around the garden or throw back one's head and laugh...

Yellow-headed Atthis, lazy-eyed, sitting on the steps of the temple ruin, wove a flower wreath for me and I wove one for her. Then, returning home, we bathed at our fountain, splashing each other, the sun on us and the slippery marble. Afterwards, we lay down and slept, and I dreamed of a ship at sea, her mast broken, her tangled sail and rigging dragging.

Will the war never end?

Fog, as grey as a shepherd's cloak, ruffled the bay for a day and a night. Then, stabbing us, came clarity, and inside that clarity, centered in it, a brown intaglio, a small wooden carving, first one ship and then another. Our fleet had sailed back to us! I watched from the terrace, unable to speak. Atthis ran up to me. Anaktoria came. Gyrinno came. Boys yelled. Old men rushed past the house. Dogs barked. Someone banged a drum. Such clamoring!

But was it joyous news, I asked myself? Why were the women in a knot at the corner? Why hadn't fast rowers raced to tell us? Had the fog tricked the fleet?

Changing my clothes, putting on new sandals, I walked to the pier and the seagulls screamed and we waited and waited. People surged all about, saying wild things, shrieking—then, ominously, fell silent. Their shouts were better than their silence. The ocean seemed too calm, as if it had been smothered by the fog or dreaded the arrival of our fleet.

I had pictured the ships as fast moving, bright on bright water.

As the first one approached, I saw no happy faces, no lifted hands, no raised shields, no plumed helmets at the rail, no flags.

I heard an oar drag and in that sound I heard the rasp of death. If Alcaeus is dead, I will take poison—and I saw myself going to Xerxes, our Persian chemist, and asking for the powder. We had agreed, years back, during another crisis, that he would allow me this gift to free myself, if I must. His yellow face vanished, as

I watched an anchor plunge slowly and saw the sail topple into the water and heard a man cry some name.

Shouts went up.

A chorus began.

Voices caught our song, way out at sea, assuring us that these were not phantoms.

Alcaeus?

Ten years ago, almost ten—ten years ago, he had left Mytilene, the wars sweeping him away. Ten years we had lived with fear creeping about our island. Ten years—how my fingers trembled. I saw those years, there on the wharf, saw them in the gulls' wings, in the distraught faces about me, my girls', my friends', my neighbors'. We had all waited for this homecoming. And now, now our fleet was gliding toward us, grey-hulked, no flags raised, oars shuffling like sick crabs.

Was it defeat or half-victory? Who, among our men, was lost, dead, or wounded? Gull on the masthead, apple at the end of the bough, what can you tell us at such crucial times? For an infinitude, the oars paced, a boat swung, another boat anchoring alongside, the armor on deck flashing, the waves gulping at the gulls.

I turned away, moved back.

And then I saw someone helping Alcaeus ashore—wounded or ill—and old, old, I thought.

Beauty said to me: This is only change.

And I said: But what is change?

And I slipped away, not daring to meet him, hoping someone would shout a name and confirm that this was another, not Alcaeus. But no, I knew. A woman knows a man she has loved, however battered he may be. I turned to watch his blundering progress.

The chorus had dwindled—only those at sea, the far off crews, still carried the hymn. I could not remain any longer. I hurried home, past his house to mine, wondering what kind of haven it could be, wondering what people would say at my flight. Yet this was not flight; it was merely a postponement, waiting for a sign, a chance to prepare myself. Alcaeus...must I send someone to him? What must I do? Go to his home? Shall I be there for him when he arrives?

At my door I turned and retraced my steps to his house, the laces of my sandals making a sound I had never heard before, the gulls wailing, the sounds from the wharf intermingling and incomprehensible.

And I was there when he came with his servant, an ugly Parthian, helping him. Yes, I was there and put out my hand to touch him, hearing his troubled breathing, seeing his torn and disheveled clothes, his rank beard, and knowing he was ill. I remembered the dream, the ship with its broken sail. And I remembered our love and I said to him:

"Alcaeus...it is I, Sappho..."

He squared his shoulders, his cloak slipping away. His arms went out to me, then dropped to his side.

His eyes had the marble core of nothingness in them.

Appalled, I could scarcely stand. O God, what is this that can happen to a man? Why has it happened? His arms in bandages, his eyes forever bandaged by the dark.

"Alcaeus..."

He heard my whisper and shuffled backwards, bumping his servant; he moved forward then and gripped me hard, twisting my flesh, his great muscles rising in his hands.

"Take me to my room... You haven't forgotten the way, have you?"

I took his arm and the Parthian opened the door and servants bowed about us; yes, I took his arm and silently we climbed the stairs to his room, his clothes rough against me, his sea smell around me. We passed his library that held the books he had loved. We passed his mother's room, where she had died. We passed where light fell around us, though no light entered his eyes.

"You are in your room," I said.

"Where?"

"Beside your Egyptian chair."

"Can I sit down on it?"

"Yes, it's ready for you."

Grasping the heavy frame, he lowered himself and the taut leather squeaked. I placed a pillow behind him and drew a fur across his knees, then sat next to him. The door had shut itself and we were alone. We listened to each other's breathing and his hand sought mine and climbed my robe to my face and the coarse fingers felt my cheek and I felt them reach my heart, with the past roaring around me like the recent storm.

I couldn't speak. I felt that the war was forever between us and I hated those years, those battles, the lines on his face. My hate was there, between us. Then, then, tears came to his eyes. Silently, he wept. And I drew him to me.

I heard the wind cross over his house.

Voices shuffled below us in the courtyard, the excited voices of the caretakers, the idle, the hangers-on. I could imagine their leers, their whispers. I lifted his face toward mine and kissed him, his heavy beard sticking my mouth.

There was a sob—a broken gasp. How ill he looked, how tired...

"You must lie down, Alcaeus. Come, I'll help you."

And when he was settled, I brought him water.

"Water...there hasn't been much water these last few days at sea..."

So he had come home, "homeward from earth's far end," on the shield of blindness. I saw him next day and the next, but he seemed strange, withdrawn. I found two of his servants but he wasn't interested.

I thought of him as old. But was he old? Age was in his scars, in his streaked hair and beard, the hands lifting and settling awkwardly.

Warm under the stars, the daphne fragrant, his sea terrace tiles smooth underneath our feet, we sat alone, some rooster vaguely saluting the night, the movement of the surf faint, almost lost. I crushed some daphne in my palm, remembering their four-pronged flowers, remembering—remembering Alcaeus after his field games, his javelin and discus throwing, his flushed face, his eyes lit, his mouth hungry for mine. Remembering—was he remembering, too?

"There was no daphne where I was," he said, his voice sullen. "It would have been better to have died there, than come home like this."

"It's spring, Alcaeus, don't talk like that," I said, and wondered what spring might signify to him.

He did not speak for a while, then quietly, as though to himself, or from another world, he repeated lines we had loved:

"The gods held me in Egypt, longing to sail for home, for I had failed to seek their blessing with an offering..."

His voice had not changed, I realized with a start. Surcharged with new meaning, it entered my being, as he went on about the galleys and the old men "deep in the sea's abyss."

The phrase haunted me because it was he who lived in an abyss.

As days passed, defeat was all that we heard in our town, not outright defeat, but capitulation—retreat combined with truce, truce necessitated by deception. Or was it confusion? The soldiers I met, after their drunken reunions, spoke of the war with bitterness. Ten years, they said. Ten years, for what? And how many of us came back? Those who had been away longest considered themselves out-casts and those who had returned during the war complained, unable to recognize their families.

Standing on the wharf, I familiarized myself with the fleet, its remnants, anchored forlornly in the bay, boys swimming around the hulls, the decks bone dry, hawsers trailing, a door off its hinges, the cordage so rotten a gull might topple a spar. Disgust in my mouth, I tasted the waste of life, Alcaeus', my own, my friends'.

What is life for, but love?

And love sent Atthis and me along the beach, stretching our legs, running, dashing in and out of shallows, finding periwinkles, the day even-tempered, goats nibbling at wild celery, their bells lazy, a fisherman waving at us as he cast his net, clouds over the mountain. I noticed Atthis against the luminous water, her fragile face trusting life. Her yellow ringlets in my lap, she sang to me and then, eyes shut, fingers in the sand, she seemed to steal away.

"What are you thinking about, darling?"

"You..."

"What about?"

"You and Alcaeus—you are so troubled for him."

"Then you have seen him?"

"Yesterday. And I'm afraid."

"Why?"

"Because what is there left for him—and you?"

"I can't answer you, Atthis. Time answers such questions."

I sense my old loneliness, a loneliness that was distorted like a ship's rib, tossed on the beach, warped because of bad luck.

"His arms have been injured, too," Atthis said.

"They will get better, in time..." And I heard time in the receding wave and felt it in her ringlets and in her hands.

"You're so sweet," she said and I saw myself mirrored in her eyes. And it occurred to me that Alcaeus and I would never again be able to exchange notes, those hasty, affectionate scribbles. Would he ever again dictate his bawdy poems, lampoon dictators and brag about war? Had pen and desk become his enemies?

Many things occurred to me, there on the sand, as Atthis and I talked softly.

Sappho's garden, terraces of roses, shrubbery and cypress,
has the ocean below: moonlit, she stands white-robed
close to marble statuary:
a nude Hermes, a bust of Aphrodite,
a niobe, an athlete from Delphi.
Sappho sits down on a bench and fingers a lyre.

*T*onight, I have returned to my poetry, for the solace and sound of my pen. Here in my library, time will be defeated for a moment, at least. The sun's last rays stream in, so yellow, they might be made of acacia. The cooling light covers my desk and bookshelves and relinquishes its hold of my vase. A fragment clings to the amphora Alcaeus gave me long ago. Its dancing, singing men seem somehow out of focus; yet it seems I hear the flute and lyre of the ceramic players.

> *I dreamed I talked with Cyprus-born...*

No, that is a poor line.
Maybe this is a better theme for tonight:

> *But I, I love delicate living, and for me,*
> *richness and beauty belong to the sun...*

There was a symposium and Gyrinno danced for the guests and afterwards brought me news about Alcaeus, how he left the party and wandered to the beach. There he quarreled with Charaxos, both armed with sticks and staggering drunk. At first, Gyrinno garbled the news, mixing it with the symposium's talk of war, the defeat, the hatreds of many kinds, including punishment and forfeit. It must have been a sorry meeting, this reunion of our warriors. Gyrinno reached me drenched with wine the men hard thrown on her. Other girls had been treated the same.

Welcome home—men!

When I had soothed Gyrinno and bathed and perfumed and powdered her, I went to the beach, thinking I might find them. Yes, they were there, quarreling on the sand, my lover and my brother, kicking their naked shins on driftwood, their servants standing by, only half interested and half awake.

"Charaxos," I began.

"Ah...I rather expected you."

"Sappho?" called Alcaeus.

"Get up, both of you." I moved past the servants indignantly.

"Just leave us alone," growled Charaxos.

"Leave a blind man with you, when it is you who is really blind?"

"Let's not resume our quarrel," said Charaxos.

"When have we stopped?"

"Please go away," said Alcaeus, "I can take care of him, myself."

"I'll not go! I intend to see you home!" And I ordered the servants to separate them and leave me with Alcaeus.

Mumbling, he followed along the shore, walking uncertainly, but keeping out of the way of the inrushing water. Where rocks littered the beach, he allowed me to help him, and was soon apologizing.

"I haven't been home a month and already I act the fool. What right have I to criticize anybody? So he brought home a slave woman. Haven't I had my share?"

I did not interrupt, preoccupied as I was with guiding him. Besides, my anger with Charaxos was too old, too deep-seated, too complex. It was not a subject to pursue on the beach, with the wind carrying our words and the breakers drowning them. This was, I preferred, a private quarrel.

With Charaxos and his men following a distance apart, we made a pretty picture, hiccoughing through Mytilene! Its silent streets were topped by a new moon; Venus seemed swallowed by a single window. Why were we in such contrast?

Laughter and outworn songs...swaying and shuffling...until the shutting of my door.

Alone, I sit beside my lamp to consider its flame, the why and wherefore of its integrity, fragility. Shadows are commonplace when we ignite a lamp. Yet, without a light, there are profounder shadows.

I hear that Alcaeus goes out alone, forbidding his servants to follow. Everyone has become uneasy.

Today, he dismissed his secretary. So poor Gogu has sought me out to explain what happened.

"Someday he will do me in. He has threatened this often enough!" He was trembling so hard, he could hardly speak. It is no wonder Alcaeus calls him a "stick of driftwood." He has an abandoned air that begs to be found and picked up.

"The least word, the least word upsets him. And you know how Alcaeus can rant!"

"Yes, well..."

"He says our great fight at Sigeum was lost through sheer carelessness. Of course, he blames the other officers..."

But then, Gogu has never held anyone's interest or respect for long. Who but Alcaeus would have hired an epileptic, in the first place? Almost everyone has rescued Gogu, at one time or another, from the surf, the wine shop, the brothel or the forum. How does this knobby skeleton manage to survive and endure?

"You will speak to Alcaeus? You promise?"

I promised. The dread of having Gogu permanently abandoned is worse than imploring Alcaeus to take him back. Besides, his scholarship is often surprising, and Alcaeus can use his help.

So later, I invited Alcaeus and some friends to supper. We sat around the courtyard fountain and listened to the harpists playing under the burning lamps. Libus, Nanno, Suidas—they are good company for Alcaeus. He seemed more like himself again, joking and talking. Again he lampooned Mimnermos and mimicked "that strange-smelling country poet from Smyrna." But I detected a morbid note, a self-hostility that cut him more than it did those he scorned.

Will he ever write again?

He left early, insisting he would find his way home by himself. A soldier, reduced to being treated like an irresponsible infant—of course he resented it. But I know he did not return home. Instead, he has rambled into the hills again.

Now the others are gone. And I wonder, looking towards the slope, what it is that Alcaeus hopes to find, a new life?

I shall not be able to sleep indoors tonight. My bed will have to be under the trees. Perhaps the wind can bring me some special message.

The banquet honoring the warriors was held last night.

Alcaeus had his collection of war shields displayed on his dining room walls. Of hide and metal, in various shapes, they united the room and its glazing lamps and candles. I felt myself the focal point of a painted eye on a circular hide, as I sat by him. I could not recall such an assembly in years: Scythian, Etruscan,

Turkish, Negro. Bowls of incense sent threads to the ceiling. Wisps floated in front of me where a man in Egyptian clothes, headband studded with rubies, sat beside his courtesan.

Alcaeus made his way to the dais, when everyone was seated, about fifty of us. Hands resting on a table, arms healed and ringed with copper bands, he leaned forward, waiting for silence. His hair had been freshly curled, and his beard trimmed and brushed with oil. I was troubled, thinking he might be impudent or truculent. Instead he spoke gravely and it was difficult to believe he could not see us. I thought he glanced straight at me.

"Tonight, friends, there will be no tirade, no poetry. I wish to pay my respects, and offer my thanks for our return to our island. I know how beautiful it is..."

There was a murmur of appreciation.

"Soldiers have a way of talking out of turn," he went on, reminding them of the gossip that had come to his ears, shameful talk that made faces blush with guilt and anger.

"It's time for me, as their commander, to speak. Very well, I will!" And his voice thundered across the room, to make sure that none would miss or mistake its message. Was this the Alcaeus who had joked and sported and sung ribald songs, as the popular friend of young men who were proud, rich, playful and naive? Here was someone speaking out of experience...

"I assure you the truce was an honorable truce—and will be respected." An older, solemn Alcaeus...who reviewed the war with wisdom.

"And now let us forget fear and enjoy life and see that our people prosper." It was an impressive speech, one they would long remember.

Our personal servants, assisted by the usual naked boys, waited on us, pouring the Chian wine. Gradually, people began to move about, to talk and drink together. Men long absent from such gatherings moved nervously or waited glumly—alone or in knots of two or three, feeling separate. How does one forget the battlefield? I heard the burr of ancient Egyptian. Persian was spoken by men from Ablas. Women gathered about the newly returned; some were excited, some were beautifully dressed, their hair piled in curls, their shoulders bare, wearing gold sandals.

As the evening wore on, the old familiar sense of freedom returned. Restraint dropped away. Voices and laughter increased. Then applause broke out as a Negro entertainer entered, carrying a smoking torch.

Under the edge of the portico, he freed a basket of birds and juggled several wicker balls. I had never seen this gaunt, ribbed giant, beautifully naked; some said he had come on a wine ship as a crewman. He spun the cages higher and higher and as they whirled in the torch light, he tore open first one and then anther, to liberate the birds. A magnificent performance.

The suggestion worried Pittakos and he pushed through the crowd to take the floor. Pittakos, with his rasping tongue and fish eyes—was there a more dishonest ruler? How ironical that he should represent us! As he kept folding and unfolding his robe, he spoke about our fleet, how he would have the ships repaired and converted into fishing boats for the use of the community...never mentioning that our fleet was rotted!

Presently, the musicians and dancers wandered among us and the party went on. After many songs and a lot of wine, Alcaeus slipped his arm through mine and suggested we go upstairs. It was all very obvious, of course—that he was drunk and I unwilling, that times had changed and everything with it. When was it we had dashed, hand in hand, up his staircase, giggling and pushing one an-other? How many years ago?

Ah, deception and illusion, do we dare recreate the past and its former happiness? Only in memory is it done successfully. Yet, here we were in his room.

Life is for love!

In the old days, when we had made love, we had closed our eyes, to intensify sensations. Now he would not need to shut his eyes. And his arms, hands, fingers—once young and sure—what could they remember?

I could not keep back tears, tears he would never know, as he stumbled, laughed, then sprawled over the fur covering of his bed. While the music filtered in to us, I cushioned him in my lap and wiped the perspiration from his face, hating the war and the years behind us. After mumbling a few words, he turned over and fell into profound sleep.

So, that was the resumption of our love...and, as I leaned against a hillside olive, the salt air fresh about me, I accepted defeat, aware that my loneliness would appear again and again. There, on the hill, gazing seaward, where fishing smacks moved, I rubbed the horny bark, envying the tree's longevity and its years ahead. Would I trade places, to brood over Mytilene, for centuries?

Alone?

Then Atthis circled me in her arms, creeping up behind me and cupping my eyes. I recognized her by her laughter and perfume.

"Atthis..."

Alcaeus' home is much older than mine, with patina walls, Parian marble floors, and a collection of rare Athenian busts. His library has a Corinthian copy of Homer and a collection of Periander's maxims, while I have been contented with some papyri, of choral lyrics and dithyrambs.

As I stretch out in a leather chair in his library and read to him, the honeysuckle makes its fragrance outside, surely a woman's flower, so fecund. I try to keep my voice and thoughts within the room, beyond the reach of its fragrance. The honeysuckle does not suit us or the room. And Alcaeus knows this, too. His impassive features grow stern, as though to reprimand me. Insatiable Sappho! Yet how can I help it? I must love and be loved.

Laying down the book, I kneel and place my cheek against his knee. His hands, gliding over my hair and neck, are dead. His voice, out of its black, reproaches me.

I want to cry: but I didn't blind you!

The other day in the library, he said:

"I wanted to write something great... During the war, I conceived of a series of island poems, bucolic, legendary, praise of this life." And he motioned toward the ocean and our island.

"Dictate to me," I said, hoping to rouse his impulse.

His silence, at first natural enough, went on, and I became embarrassed by his stare at the bookshelves.

"I want to help you, Alcaeus."

Again the silence. How was I to get through it?

Taking a volume of his poems, I read aloud several of his favorites. Slowly, his face relaxed and he settled deeper in his chair. After a while, he said:

"Read some of yours, Sappho."

I opened a book, one of my earliest ones, and read several passages. But I could not continue; I felt my mind wrapped in fog; my hands became icy. I shut my eyes and said to myself: See, this is what it's like to be blind. You're blind,

blind to love and life...

As I kissed him good-bye, I longed for our youth, its freedom, its daring, its quarrels and fun.

Walking home, I told myself I should never return to his house.

In looking back over the pages of my journal, I am alarmed by the passage of time. When I was young, I thought time was a philanthropist.

I remember so well that day mama took me to the ocean, and the rain fell unexpectedly, lashing and soaking us. We finally discovered a shepherd's hut, but I got colder and colder in its windowless gloom. Lying on the floor, among stiff hides, with the rain sounding loud and the hides smelling strong, I thought the storm would never end. Toward dusk, a shepherd and his boy came, dripping with wet and shivering, and my mother dried the boy and made him lie down with me under the hides. Were we seven or eight? Together, our bodies grew warm and we lay still, listening to the wind and the rain thud across the green roof, while the shepherd went about building a fire and preparing supper. I have forgotten the boy's name, but not his face. Forever after, I thought of him as my first lover. I doubt whether we spoke a word all that delicious evening.

Now I find it hard to renew ties with the past. Not only Alcaeus...but Dioscurides...Pylades...Milo...the very names make me unhappy. All destroyed by war. What special stupidity do men possess that they must involve themselves in such a gamble, with loss inevitable, anyhow?

The columns of the temple of Zeus, in Athens,
stand white against the moonlit sky.
A woman walks among columnar cypress,
her sandals scraping sand and gravel.
A hawk wheels above.

he masks I have on my bedroom walls seem less clever than they appeared years ago. Our theatre, too, has changed through the years, become more mediocre.

Yesterday, at the play, I sat closer than usual and was delighted by the comic faces, so new and frightful that children screamed and squealed. Good, I thought. Perhaps the play may take on life.

...A man with a tambourine strutted about...an old beggar, pack on back, pulled at his beard and mimicked words sung by the chorus. He seemed to be one of us or a Chian, maybe. It was pleasant enough to soak myself in comedy for a while, for right after the play, Charaxos found me and suggested we stroll in private. Obviously, he had something on his mind!

He began by offering me an exquisite scarab, saying he had purchased it for me, from a sailor who had touched port.

"For me?" I became suspicious! I fingered the beetle-shaped oval, unlike any I had seen. An amethyst was set in the center with characters engraved around it.

"An Etruscan scarab should make a pretty keepsake," he said.

"Then I think you should keep it."

"Why? Are you afraid?" he asked.

"Of what?"

"That it might bring bad luck."

He laughed ironically, as he flipped and caught the scarab, with a flick of his wrist.

"What is it you want?" I asked, coming directly to the point.

"To be treated with respect, Rhodopis and I—not criticized."

"Do I say too much?"

"I don't like your tongue." He was scowling now.

"Nor I your woman's!"

"Leave her out! I warn you—she's no longer a slave!"

"It wasn't that she was a slave that bothered me."

"A courtesan, then!"

"No, you should know better than that. Oh, no...it was your assumption that our family funds could be lifted, without my consent and without my knowledge. Taken to buy Rhodopis. You sold three or four wine ships to pay her price, along with the money taken from me."

"Can't you forget..."

"Not conveniently. Nobody enjoys being robbed."

"I have said I would repay you."

"But that was nearly two years ago. And you go right on selling wine and buying equipment. I have heard that you added a ship last month. Wasn't it convenient to pay me then?"

His fist tightened over the scarab, and he bowed and turned away, rejoining his wife who was strolling behind us with her friends and servants.

Theatre!

Villa Poseidon

Atthis, Gyrinno, Anaktoria and I went swimming in the bay by the driftwood tree. It was late, the sun misty, its eye sleepy, pelicans roosting, a dolphin or two frolicking close to shore. I had been unable to forget my meeting with Charaxos, until Anaktoria, who is the best swimmer among us, grabbed me by the heels as I floated by, and towed me to the bottom. That ended my anger and irritation. I lit after her, snatching for her long hair. Arms around her, I forced her to tow me toward shore, making myself as heavy as possible.

As the four of us played on the beach, I thought: When will this happen again? Something about the late afternoon—its hammered out sun, its tempered air, its windlessness, its smell of spring—seemed unreal even as it happened. We tossed our blankets on the sand, dashed back and forth to the water's edge, splashed each other, then arranged ourselves in a circle and began combing each other's hair. We sang and laughed, comparing, whose was finest, whose was thickest.

Atthis, whose hair was shortest, bragged she could swim the farthest. That started an argument.

"Who swam halfway round the island last year?" demanded Gyrinno.

"Who was born at sea?" said Anaktoria.

"You can tell the best swimmer by the shape of her buttocks," said Atthis. "Look at mine, how flat they are." She jumped up, to show us.

"A boy's buttocks," laughed Gyrinno.

"Here. Measure. Mine are smaller," said Anaktoria.

So we measured, laughing, fussing, pushing, our hair streaming around us—a gull on the shore padding back and forth, scolding. Atthis won, but Anaktoria had the loveliest breasts, so round, almost transparent in that evening light. I have rarely seen a girl of such grace, not the childish grace of some, but the accomplished grace of true femininity. As the others became aware of my admiration, they became jealous and peevish, and tried to shift the praise.

They talked about my smallness, my violet hair... "your deep blue eyes"... "your melodious voice..."

But this was Anaktoria's hour. She had been away, visiting in Samnos, staying with her family, and I was eager to hear the news.

"I thought I was homesick... But it is Mytilene I love best... My brother has a girl now. He goes to her house whenever he is not working. I saw very little of him... Life there was very dull. Family visits from door to door. The same cup of wine, the same paste of nuts and fruit, the same questions, answers, family anecdotes and jokes... How lonesome I was!"

Growing quiet, all of us responded to the evening, the lingering sea-light, the arrival of the stars, the whispering shingle, the breeze, carrying the scents and sounds from Mytilene.

Anaktoria and I walked home together, feeling our bond closer, stronger than before. I had missed her more than I thought: I had missed her a dozen times a day.

I have been sick today and to amuse myself I have made some jottings about my girls:

Atthis—lover of yellow ribbons, scared of the dark. To avoid going out, will invent a headache, a toothache or a stomachache. An orphan, she gets homesick for the home she never had. Prefers women to men. Tells amusing jokes and stories. Loves laughter. Mimics. Is made jealous easily. Speaks slowly...ivory-skinned.

Gyrinno—the daughter of a wine merchant, can outdrink most men. Worries about her figure, eats next to nothing. Uses violet perfume. Our best dancer. Otherwise, is lazy, careless of dress and makeup. Never reads. Wants to marry someone wealthy and entertain lavishly. Snores.

Anaktoria—hair yellower than torchlight, soft-girl, dabbler in poetry, dreamer, lovely singer. Plays lyre and flute equally well. Adores games, trees, flowers, swimming, archery. Wants to travel, be a priestess.

Then there are the new girls: Heptha, with copper hair... Myra, who is Turkish... Helen, a scatterbrained darling... Ah, but each is exquisite in her own way. No two are alike. I love them all.

And yet, I am grieved, since my own daughter is jealous of them. Dear, foolish Kleis, who pretends she has never been a child and is yet so far from being a woman.

I have spent weeks over a poem, revising, revising.

I do my best writing in the morning, when the sea light is sparking my room. How important the harmony is to me: harmony in my house, on the island, in my heart.

Sometimes, I call my girls to let them hear what I have written. Sometimes, in the evenings, I recite my poems for friends. Sometimes, I go days, unable to write a word. They are cold days.

Shall I use eleven syllables?

A poem does not grow like a leaf, but has to be shaped. I often think of a lyric as an amphora; little by little I must mold its lines on the wheel of my mind. It is the structure, containing the song. It must be graceful, strong, so that the words and the music can flow...

> *The wings of the swans have drawn you toward the dark ground,*
> *with yoke chariot bearing down from heaven...*
> *Come to me...free me from trouble...*

Today I received a letter from Aesop, written at Adelphi. It is a joy to hear from him. I thought he had forgotten me. What a good companion he was, all those days in Corinth... Companion? He was more like a father!

His handwriting is the most perfect I have ever seen. Each letter formed so patiently, each thought expressed so beautifully. Does he strive for perfection because be cannot forget his deformity?

I remember his eyes used to transfix me with their brown hypnosis.

He must be fifty, I think.

He had his beard trimmed and his hair curled, every morning. His robes, so elegant, so clean, were always perfumed. I seldom saw him without his doll, that bull-leaping doll of Cretan ivory, brightly painted! But his apartment was simple, tastefully furnished, elegant as his clothes. Each bath towel, I recall, bore a brilliant red octopus.

When he looked after Alcaeus and me, we ate with him every day at least one meal. Through all the years of our exile, he remained our most faithful friend. His friends were our friends. His house was ours. His servants. He treated everyone with equal respect.

"I never forget that I was a slave," he often said.

He was much sought after, not only for his humor, but for his wisdom. His reddish whiskers and black brows gave him a comic look. But he sensed his profundity, as he guided me about Corinth and sat beside me at the temple of Apollo, watching the people and the boats and the sea birds, and hearing the choral virgins sing.

Evenings, he would lay aside his doll and tell me fables. He had learned many from his father, a Persian, and he was constantly visiting orientals to pick up their stories and jokes. I hear his smooth, somnolent voice...an effortless storyteller!

"I will certainly come and visit you," he writes. "I am tired of Adelphi. The people make me uncomfortable. I want to roam over Lesbos, to be with you and Alcaeus. I want to see your home."

Will he come? I hope he can. His letter has taken weeks to reach me. I suppose he could be on his way, by this time.

It must have been almost dawn, when Alcaeus and a group of revelers came banging at my door, shouting, laughing. We let them in and they demanded breakfast, some of the more intoxicated trying to seduce my girls, who were quite amused.

When the others were gone, Alcaeus drew me aside to speak in earnest.

"Do you know that Kleis goes to Charaxos' house?"

"What do you mean by that?"

"That she visits your brother's house frequently."

"Do you know this...or is it gossip?"

"We just went by his place. She's there now. I would know her voice anywhere."

"Yes, of course..."

"I don't like his slaves, as you know, and I don't think they are fit company for Kleis."

"No, no, certainly, I shall speak to her..."

"It will take more than that, I'm afraid."

"Why, Alcaeus, she's a mere child..."

"Oh come now, Kleis must be fourteen or more. If she were my daughter, a pretty girl..." He held up a warning finger, then left.

Fourteen? No doubt he meant well, was sincere, but I resented the implication.

Have I really been lax? Is my little girl in need of direction? It seems she was ten or eleven only yesterday. Fourteen, indeed!

Kleis never knew her father. He is one of a thousand dead, because of the wars. If he were here, she would not think of slipping off at night. She looks much like him. I remember his face, the candid eyes and lips.

I remember the ivory gleam of his body. Ah, if he were here...

How am I to forbid Kleis?

Where is my frivolity? Where is my enthusiasm?

The sun's color whitened my shutters and I threw them open on the sea and the light burnished the tiles and splashed the masks and my bed and I stared into its eye, to surprise its oracle.

I am criticized for my simple dress, my tastes. The townspeople say I should not be aloof. They say I am too aristocratic. They say my parties are too gay and exclusive. They say my wealth is insufficient. They say...Yes, I could go on with this pettiness. But why should I?

I have my work and I must live to see beyond the moment, below the surface; I must interpret the whole heart. For I know too well the inexorability of time, the disappointments that nibble one's heels. I must offset the pain, the loss. There is no one to take my arm, there is no one to lean on. There is only my work—and my girls.

All day in the fragrant lemon forest, fallen fruit underneath the trees...all day alone. I have hated loneliness and yet I must be able to rest and get away from responsibilities, to welcome the gods of trees and ocean and those long dead, whose marble shrines dot a corner of this wood. There are so many dead. However, life must be better than death or the gods would have chosen to die. Life must be day-by-day and hour-by-hour. And I talk to myself and totally convince myself and then the mew of a gull shatters my conviction.

Our spring revel saw us high on the mountain, the ocean misty blue, our erotic flutes wailing the dawn. Kleis and I danced together, my girls joining us one by one, the deepest notes growing in volume, the slight notes dropping away. How the wet grass slid our feet!

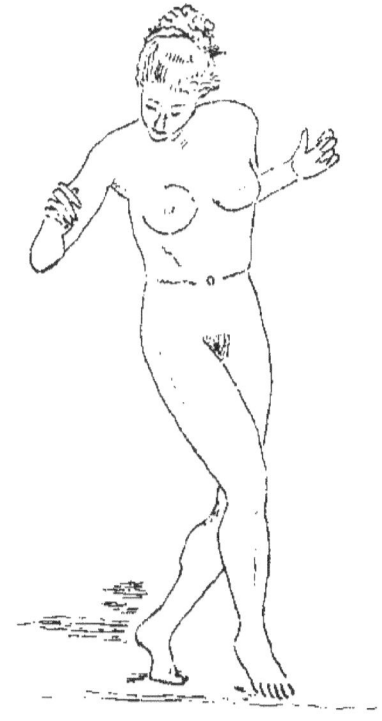

I closed my eyes, remembering nothing, letting the song have me; then, eyes open, I went on forgetting, forgetting where I was, what this was: I was simply dancing, flashing with someone, alone, dancing for myself and the oncoming sun, dancing because I love to dance, dancing because I love life and time is dead. Yes, time is dead at our spring festival and the flowers never spill from our hair.

Girls bared their breasts and arms to the light. Men clapped in unison. The music sped up and the faster pace widened our circle of dancers. Our bare feet kicked blossoms thrown by boys. We ate and danced, drank and danced again. Kleis, it seemed to me, danced more beautifully than anyone.

Beauty, I said: We are here again, help

us to find life's meaning.

Beauty said: There is always meaning, look for it.

The step and re-step, circle and re-circle, gulp of air, ache of chest, ache of legs and arms, sullen eyes, eyes longing for embrace...longing... longing...isn't that what life is?

Our tumbled-down temple rose behind us, whitish pillars, roofless phalli, our gowns, arms and faces, circling.

Through my blur of happiness, I saw Anaktoria, Libus, Gorgo, Nano, old friends, fishermen, villagers. Old women went about hawking oranges. Old men drank and talked.

In the afternoon, resting under trees, I became aware that the crowd had scattered into small groups. How hungry we were! How thirsty! Then more dancing and, with tiny fires in the twilight, food cooking, pots bubbling, love-making, songs. It was the dusk I love. And it was easy to grow sentimental, to talk of Alcaeus and miss him, to remember our fun at other festivals. Crickets bubbled like little pots. Frogs burped. A bat fluttered over our fires. Below, somewhere on the bay, a ship winked and made me feel that the sky had gotten below us.

A warm wind and some scarves, that was all I needed to sleep, a sleep some-what troubled because Kleis was not with me. But during the night she appeared and slipped into my arms, where she began to cry. I comforted her and slept and thought no more about her girlish tears till morning, when she whispered about Charaxos, his heavy drinking, then the darkness and torches, the wild games and dances higher up the mountain...

"I shouldn't have gone with him! I should have stayed with the other boys and girls right here. This time, he has changed me. I'll never be the same! And I can't bear the sight of him!"

...A journal is for solace, for strength.

I write in my library, the rain falling, Kleis in her room, asleep. How sad when youth is tricked! One speaks of treachery, stupidity, ugliness. One thinks of family honor. And then I realize that Charaxos has no sense of honor, that my code is incomprehensible to him. So, I'll not show my distress—our distress.

Life is for the strong, they say.

How strong must a person be?

I feel like dry smoke. And smoke twists and turns inside, not knowing which way to go. Nothing is hotter than the heat of anger.

Charaxos—how the name burns my tongue, sears my tablet. It is impossible to concentrate!

It wasn't enough for us to quarrel over money! You, with your scarab, your Egyptian clothes, your obelisks, your slaves, your woman!

Perhaps Kleis is mistaken. Children are given to exaggeration.

I don't know what to believe.

Today, an earthquake shook our island, sloshing water from our courtyard fountain, making birds cry out. As the walls of the house trembled, I shut my eyes, thinking: No, not yet...there's still so much.

And I made up my mind to go out more, to get about more. With Kleis. We need more time together.

How tall she is! With golden hair and mint eyes, she grows more like her father each day. I detect a restlessness in her nature. Is it because of what happened, or because she is with me? Or do I imagine it?

Her shoulders stoop, her face is sad. When I speak to her about it, she straightens and gazes far off, her eyes worried. Perhaps we make a strange pair.

Gems:
A horseman on a gold agate,
a Nike on chalcedony,
a nude girl on jasper,
a fighting lion on rock crystal...
Sappho is enjoying her collection:
the sun, in her bedroom, is all white.
She is all white.
The gems flash:
We see Sappho's face in her hand mirror,
the faces of her girls around her,
girls singing.

O ne of my girls has had a birthday. It should have been a happy day. There were garlands, songs, dances... Then, someone came to me, brimming with the amusing story: Kleis has been heard to say that she doesn't know how old she is!

"I've had so many double birthdays, I've lost count," were the words repeated to me.

Why do we wish to be older, younger, always in protest? Why are we never satisfied?

I wish there were no birthdays.

For several days, Kleis and I have sailed, our boat a good fishing boat, captained by a young man named Phaon.

It was our first excursion around the whole island, in years. We sailed past Malea Point to Eresos, to Antiss, then Methymn, and round our island, back to Mytilene. I have never seen the water so calm. Probably because of the recent hot spell, the captain said.

What a peaceful island, our Lesbos... We saw Mt. Ida, olive groves, cypress, temples, bouldered shores, goatherds, date palms, sailboats, dolphins... We thought of Odysseus, trying to identify ourselves with that heroic past, we—only islanders enjoying a holiday!

A striped awning sheltered us during the hot hours of the day. Nights were cool and comfortable. Our handsome captain was attentive. I thought he was particularly agreeable. Our food was tasty. How time drifted along.

Of course it was our being together, lulled by the sea, that made the trip so happy for Kleis and me. It was our shared regrets, our resolve for the future, that brought us close. It was the little things we did for one another, the sleeping together...the voiceless communication.

How wonderful it is to get out of bed and stand by the window and take in the sea and breathe deeply.

How good it is to dream a little.

Phaeon...it is such a beautiful name.

There are days when my girls seem utterly listless. Their activities have no meaning to them. Nothing pleases them. I hear them arguing among themselves, apart. It is as though a stranger had come to be with them.

And Kleis seems more withdrawn. Does she resent the others or do they resent her? A curious unease creeps about the place.

Sometimes, I wonder whether it is I who lacks.

I do not feel well.

Time is slipping by...

I don't know what to do about Kleis: she goes off by herself, and does not tell me where she goes. I can't very well send someone to check on her. That's an ugly thing to do.

I think she isn't visiting Charaxos' house, because he has sailed for Egypt on one of his wine ships. Of course she could be seeing someone else.

Is it possible that she is interested in Phaon...how shall I find out?

I met him on the pier, the wind blowing, the water choppy under grey skies. He left off caulking his boat with a cheery "Hello" and climbed onto the pier. How pleased he was to see me! Was I planning another trip?

Sitting on piles of rope, he told me of an underwater city he had seen, with a great bronze statue of Poseidon by a temple...

"The water was like glass, not a seaweed moving, not a current..." His hand swept sideways, spread flat. "Oh yes, coral...and plenty of fish, big ones. I swam halfway down to the city, but there was no air in me to swim deeper. A fish watched me, from one side of Poseidon, its body curving behind the statue. Poseidon's eyes were made of jewels..."

Phaon is a handsome young man: I think a man is a man when he is handsome all over. I measured him with my eyes, as he talked to me. I measured his feet, hands, thighs, shoulders—the symmetry is unusual. His skin is the color of oakum and his muscles glide perceptibly under his skin. He smells of the sea.

I stayed a long while, talking on the piles of rope, exciting talk. What would it be like to swim with him? To dive deep with him?

We talked and talked. He never mentioned Kleis. And I forgot why I came.

I went to Alcaeus, to tell him about the submerged city.

"You mean Helike?" he asked. "A quake tore apart the coast and it went under," he said, and described something of what I had heard.

"Phaon says the city is visible when the water's clear, and still," I said.

"Phaon?"

"Yes, you remember, the captain who took me on a trip around the island..."

"He fixed his sightless eyes on me and I felt stunned, as one hypnotized. I trembled. Then his expression altered and he changed the subject as quickly as a man might draw a sword during battle.

"I never thought I'd be blind. I never memorized any faces. My home, our bay, the ships—I can't recall things at will, with certainty. There's so little difference now between sleeping and waking. Anything may come to mind.

"A soldier stares at his hand, slashed by a spear. He can't believe he's wounded. It's not his blood spattering the rocks...

"A man lies beside his shield, a hole in his side. He can't believe he sees what he sees..."

Mytilene

For several days, I have been working with Alcaeus in his library. He has taken heart, at last, and is pouring out words, political invective. I sit, amazed. Even his dead eyes have gathered light. He jabs out phrase after phrase, juggling his agate paperweight from hand to hand, steadily, slowly. I barely have time to write. He breathes deeply, his voice sonorous.

Facing the sea, afternoon light on his face, he could be my old Alcaeus.

Thasos brought us wine.

And we worked still late, our lamps guttering in the wind, the air rough from the mainland, tasting of salt. Shutters groaned.

"To strike a balance between common sense and law, this is the cause to which we must pledge ourselves. Our local tyrants must go. They realize there isn't enough corn. Poverty, we must grind against poverty. If our established life and prosperity can't be made to serve, they, too, will go..."

Walking home, I was hardly aware that a gale had sprung up. Exekias, carrying my cloak, seemed surprised at my singing.

A note from Rhodopis—naturally, I was astonished. Her note concerned Kleis: could we talk together?

It was hard to order my thoughts. Rhodopis writing to me, especially with Charaxos gone...

I fixed an hour and we met at a discreet distance from the square, a bench in the rear of a small temple.

Despite the extravagant clothes, the careful makeup, how hard the eyes, the mouth. And I wondered how I looked to her, in my simple dress. But Rhodopis knows the sister of Charaxos is not naive.

It was a brief meeting, cold, the matter quickly attended to.

After waving her servants to stand apart, she faced me with unveiled scorn:

"You daughter's visits are making my household a difficult one," she said.

I flushed.

"So the plaintiff has become the accused? An interesting reversal," I murmured.

"I will expect thanks," she said, with a mocking smile, twisting her parasol into the sand, "for sparing you public embarrassment."

I knew she was sharpening her wits, and paused. She lifted a scented handkerchief to her mouth and took a slow breath.

"I have waited a long time for this, but I'm more charitable than you think. I won't keep you waiting. It is Mallia—a servant boy, who has caught Kleis' fancy..."

Vaguely, I had the flash of an image: a fair, slim, country boy, not one of the slaves.

"And what is it you want?" I said, in the same level voice.

The parasol twirled.

"Oh, things could be arranged..."

I did not doubt this. But not knowing the relationship between Kleis and Mallia, remained silent. My silence seemed to exasperate Rhodopis.

"Of course, you could send Kleis to a *thiase* in Andros," she exclaimed. I refused to flinch. Sending one's daughter to school elsewhere was to admit one's own school had failed. Rhodopis knew this, as well as I.

"Or, I could dismiss Mallia, but then, where would the lovers meet? And if he took her home with him..."

I still waited. Somewhere there was a trap. Rhodopis had not written, then met me, without a purpose.

"Perhaps you have given too much thought to family honor, Sappho. So critical of Charaxos...of me." Her voice had grown confidential.

"If Kleis has done anything foolish, I am willing to accept the responsibility," I said.

"And the consequence, too...with my husband?"

I stood up, brushing off the bench dust.

The interview was over: obviously, further discussion was useless. Why let Rhodopis press her advantage? I nodded and left, with the sound of her laughter behind me.

Why?

It is a question I must answer: it is a multiple question.

Has Rhodopis done this to spite me, wound me, shame me?

Is Kleis doing this to assert herself, to prove that she is not a child? In protest, against me, my house? To estrange us farther?

Did Kleis tell the whole truth about that day at the spring-revel? If I knew what happened...

She seemed so happy on our ocean trip. Or was it I who was happy? Perhaps I teased her too much before Phaon. Did she think I had no right to be attracted to him? Do I make her out to be more sensitive than she really is?

Love is a jealous companion.

Right now, all I can see clearly is that perfumed handkerchief and twirling parasol.

I have never been afraid of consequences attached to my own actions. Must one learn to be braver than that? Or is this a matter of impersonal wisdom?

I have sent for Kleis...

It is true she is fond of Mallia, the boy acting as guardian to her in the house of Charaxos, protecting her from Charaxos.

It was Mallia who served as wine boy at the spring festival.

Curiously, it is Rhodopis who has sided with them in opposing and blocking Charaxos. Yet, that is not so curious, either.

"You're wrong to distrust Rhodopis," says Kleis.

But my doubts persist and I consider her a foolish child. For why would she make a confidante of Rhodopis?

"I wish you could be happier with me," I said.

Our talk seemed to unlock her heart and she burst into tears and I learned how much of a child she is. For it is still filial jealousy that makes her difficult. She cannot bear to share me with my girls, my friends, even my work.

Poor, darling Kleis, how hard it is for some of us to grow up, to learn to walk gracefully alone. I kissed and comforted her as best I could, assuring her of my love.

"There's a place for you here, Kleis. Please try to find it. I know the girls are eager to help you, if you'll let them."

She promised, but the far-away look remained in her eyes.

A *thiase* in Andros—the thought saddens me, for then she would be far away.

I have hurled myself into work. During long silences, while I am thinking, composing, I hear the water clock outside my door. Drop after drop, it fastens itself to my memory.

The wind has continued for days on end, the sun hazy, the surf magnificent in its wildness, all craft beached, no gulls anywhere, a sense of abandonment throughout our town, people scurrying to get indoors.

Only in the garden is there shelter, near the fountain. An angle of the house shuts off the strongest blasts.

I have ordered everyone to work. At least they appear busy.

While the wind howled, a tempest rose in me.

I woke during the night to fight it. Yet, there it was, that perfect symmetry, stripped to the waist, brown caulking material in his hands. I did not need to light a lamp. I had memorized his body. We were moving toward the submerged city; I saw myself swimming beside him; in the water, he was above me, then below me; then we were one, diving together.

I have fought other storms in my blood, and yet this one, with the wind howling, the surf beating, threatens to overcome me. I have never felt more deserted. Death and blindness have made my bed sterile.

Beauty, stay with me! I said.

Beauty said: Don't be afraid.

How shall I cope with this whirlwind? What does it know of surfeit, satiety?

I'm too old, compared to his twenty or twenty-two. He may have a woman of his own, a country girl, a young, simple, laughing slip of a thing who satisfies him.

In my dream I saw him at the prow of his boat, talking with Kleis.

I should send her to Andros.

I need to go to Andros, myself!

I must seek Alcaeus...he must help me...

I see Phaon in his bed, his young arms, his young legs, his close-cropped hair, blue eyes, smooth face.

Like a storm punishing the olives, love shakes me.

I must go to sleep.

Forget!

Another letter has reached me from Aesop. Still in Adelphi, he writes he has been sick with fever.

"My consolation is that I am sick for good reasons. I am sick of men being mistreated. I am sick of injustice.

"As you know, I have been more than a fly on a chariot wheel. I have spoken out publicly and this has raised dust and stones. People stare at me on the streets.

"I am sick of the aristocrats. I am sick of prejudice and ignorance. There must be a better life.

"A free society...this is the most fabulous joke of all time. The ones who rant loudest about it would run the farthest, were it to happen.

"I may have to flee soon, back to Corinth, it seems. These rulers here have friends. They know how to apply pressure.

"Write me, Sappho. I need your sense of the gracious. Beauty foremost—I wish I could think as you think.

"Tell Alcaeus I send him my best, that I miss him..."

I took my letter to Alcaeus and read it aloud in his library.

"I'm afraid it is serious this time," I said.

"It is always serious, when we speak out," said Alcaeus, laying his palms flat on the desk.

"He says it is dangerous for him to come here."

"He must learn restraint!"

"And you, Alcaeus, do you think you have learned restraint?"

There was silence and then he said:

"Those of us who are free must speak, or there will be no freedom, no free men left to restrain those who think in terms of chains."

Sitting in the square the other day, I listened to Alcaeus speaking, excited because he had taken cudgel in hand. Blind though he is, he strikes an imposing figure, even majestic. Leaning on his cane, staring over the townsmen who crowd the forum, he looks a pillar, his head shaggy, beard glistening with oil, clothes immaculate.

Something about the day had a timeless quality, as though none of it was old, the exorbitant taxes, the stringent laws, the situation of the veteran—and the sea rolling, the gulls crying, the sun shining.

Pittakos has not shown any noticeable objection. Perhaps he remembers the youthful champion, before the exile. Then, it was not easy to ignore the charges against those in office, the outcries against "drunkards, thieves, bastards!" Now Pittakos nods and walks on his way, aware that a blind man may be an excellent orator but no longer a soldier.

And recalling the years in exile, I knew how bitter Alcaeus was. If there is less vehemence in his voice than before, there is also greater conviction.

Aegean shells, beach shells,
shells in a woman's hands,
shells in a child's hands.
Underwater, fish glide
through a sunken ship,
passing huge wine jars,
a young Hermes,
sponges...coral...kelp...sharks.

lcaeus has taken back his former secretary. I am glad for all our sakes: Alcaeus', Gogu's, mine. I hear they are working hard. Now, when Thasos inquires at my door, I make excuses. They can get along without me.

I keep hoping and waiting someone else will come to inquire, will bring a message. Since he never looks for me, I must not look for him.

I will walk by the sea until I am too tired to move.

My pretty Gyrinno is sick with too much sun and too much swimming so I go about pampering her and nothing pleases her more.

It has been some time since I brought her a tray, one I fixed especially for her. I combed her hair tonight, cooled her skin with ointment, and teased her till she made me promise a gift, a silver mirror from Serfo's shop, one with suitably naughty figures on the back and handle: "the convivialists," Serfo has named it.

To help pamper Gyrinno, we had musicians in the courtyard. The air was so warm, so languid, nobody wished to go to sleep. These were wandering musicians, from neighboring islands, and their songs were mostly new to us. They repeated the ones we liked best, tender mountain airs.

Kleis, who has a phenomenal memory, was able to join them the second or third time, harpist and flutist accompany. It was an intimate evening, ending with a tale by one of the wanderers, of Pegasus winging over the ocean on an errand of mercy for a lost lover.

Toward dawn, I woke to find Atthis with me, her cheek against mine. More aware of my inner needs than others, she had come to comfort me, alleviate my longing. Her perfume, kisses and caresses were not the crude, male love I wanted. However, I was half in my dreams and I remembered the music and the tale and the moonlight, our songs and voices, and everything blended into a pattern of peace and goodness.

There are times when our hearts are particularly open to beauty: this was one of those times. Everything, at this moment, assumed perfection. And because we recognize its illusory quality it is the more precious.

Out of the night comes the word someone has tried to communicate, that we are plural, not single...not forgotten. Here, in this comparison, are strength and courage.

Yes, there are times when our hearts open.

There is more to life than wandering over an island. There is more to life than happiness. There is more to life than work. There is more to life than hope. What is it?

Under a cypress, above the sea, facing the sea, I asked myself this question and found this answer:

Certainly, the living is all: there is no life after death: and since there is no other chance than this chance, it must be enough to have beauty and kindness and time to enjoy them.

Here, on this slope, earth's form assures me this is true. And at home, among my girls, I can find it so, each girl an affirmation.

Why is Kleis involved in spats with Gyrinno, Helen, Myra? Why are the girls put out with her? Why can't they agree to do the same thing at the same time?

Why is there so much unrest and dissatisfaction everywhere? Corinth, Sparta, Argos, Sicyon...the news reaches us by boat.

Why is Phaon far at sea, headed for Byzantium?

It seems to be a world of questions.

When I think how many gods exist, I am shocked by man's confusion and gullibility.

"Man is like a cricket. He sees the cricket's limitations but not his own. The cricket can't read or write or think scientifically. He can't sail a boat or build a house. He potters away in his clod or field. What can a cricket know about god?"

That's what man says, unable to see beyond his own clod. He scoffs and sneers but what is he but a two-legged cricket, brown, yellow or black? I'm sure the cricket has his illusions, some of them as pat as ours.

Charaxos has returned to Mytilene.

Our meeting was unavoidable, of course. He had on the commonplace mask of the man in the street and talked about his trip, the grinding poverty in Egypt, the bad state of our mercenaries there...

No mention of settling his debts! Not a word about Rhodopis! Evidently Kleis does not exist.

"All of us are well, thank you," I said. "Nothing has changed for us here."

What is there between us? It is something deeper than ourselves. When I walked away, my eyes burned and my cheeks felt hot.

Here is a passage from my first journal, written in childish hand:

Today is my birthday and mother gave me earrings and papa gave me a brooch with a carnelian stone. We had a party on the beach and papa burnt his fingers in the fire as we cooked the mutton meat. I don't like mutton meat. I don't like smoky fires. Papa sings badly. My dog got sick.

I suppose all that was very important to me.
Is our life important to anyone else?

No word from Aesop.

Sometimes I have to get away from everything and everyone, myself as well.

I went to a nearby fishing village. Necessity can be ingenious. The fishermen have managed to build good boats out of the battered wrecks that littered our shores. They tell me that the exporting of sponges has become extensive.

I wish I could sail with a sponge crew. I went with a crew once. Glued inside my decorum, I can't believe I was free...wild...bold...headstrong...long ago.

Yes, I would like to cruise into deep blue water and stare down, then to the sponge shallows and swim down, down.

My new book is ready.

It was interesting to visit the Kamen house and check the copies.

I stopped for a moment in the alley to gaze at the sun symbol painted over the house door. More and more, geometric designs are giving way to more plastic ideas in decorating. Polychrome painting seems to grow more imaginative. Our ceramics are becoming more forceful. I thought of these things as I looked at the sun symbol, done in blue and gold.

The Kamen brothers were, as always, mysterious, stiff, like Egyptian clay long dried by the sun. It is too bad they can't apply some of their art to themselves. They are such emaciated creatures, I wonder what they eat?

Each waits for the other to speak; each scrapes, bows, tries to efface himself. Tall, nut brown, with hair tied behind their necks, deer skin aprons over faded clothes, they make me feel like an intruder.

As for my book, it is excellently made. The brothers are perfectionists in their craft. To them, poetry is nothing. Do they read it at all? However, the libraries will be pleased to receive these copies.

I am sure this is my best work.

Thousands of white herons flew over our island this morning, making the sky a sky of motion. They flew almost all morning, flying toward the mainland. I watched them from a bridge in town, leaning against the cool stone rail, Anaktoria watching with me, perplexed. Not a bird faltered. What directed them? Not a sound, as they flew. Some of the townsmen gathered to stare, dead silent. In tens and twenties, they flew over and onward, apparently at the same speed. Twice the flocks covered the sun and our town darkened, tiled roofs turning grey.

There were murmurs...

I remembered the herons as I tried to rest, wings and more wings, bearing me away.

Sometimes, we troop to our old theatre, lost in its bowl of cypress and over-grown with grass and weeds, seats and benches crumbled. Laying aside our clothes, we toss rover reeds, have a try at archery, play catch. Or we race or go in for leap-frog or tug-of-war.

Little boys like to pester us and poke fun. Little boys—how delightful they can be.

If the day is sultry, we loll. Usually, the complaint is "too much sun." I used to think we needed lots of sun and exercise but now I'm not sure.

Lying on a moss-topped stone, time seemed to pause: I think there is trouble brewing. I don't put it past Rhodopis to concoct something. Even Kleis has been too alarmed to return to Charaxos' house. Mallia has told her to wait.

There has been a to-do because the "right" people did not attend the home-coming party for Charaxos. What a pity! I know of no changes in the life of Mytilene that required a unanimous celebration.

"Why must there be bad feelings between their house and ours?" Kleis has asked. "Of course I hate him for what he did to me."

My knees trembled.

How explain life to one who has not lived it!

"You could help me, if you wanted to," she said.

Just like that!

I believe we only know what life gives us: can sound be described to the deaf?

"After all, Charaxos is your brother," she reminded me.

I wanted to say: He was, before all, not after all.

I can barely check my anger, angers, one on top the other, too many for me to consider and come through sane.

As I went home, I saw a man beating his slave. The slave, who has had eve-rything taken from him, is being punished publicly for an insignificant theft!

The situation is becoming impossible: Why has Charaxos dragged Alcaeus into our quarrel?

I found them hurling insults at one another, Alcaeus' house and servants in an uproar. I hurried into the library and had to pound on the door.

"I can thank you for this!" shouted Charaxos, the moment he saw me.

"Leave, Sappho. I asked him to come and now I'll have him thrown out," Alcaeus bawled, lunging across the table.

"Our hero!" snorted Charaxos.

"Enough. Get out!"

"Suppose you and I have a private word elsewhere," said Charaxos to me, bitterly. "As for you, old battle ax, I'll settle with you another time. I'm sick of your trouble-making. Maybe one exile was not enough..."

Quick as a flash, I slapped him. He eyed me grimly, then turned and left.

Naturally, Alcaeus refused to tell me what the visit was about.

All this is contemptible.

I can not forget the scene of the angry men, the threat.

Perhaps the next move had better be mine? Before my opponent makes it a "check" from which I can't escape...as they say in the new Persian game.

My girls sense that I am troubled and try to distract me.

"No work today!" cries Gyrinno.

"Let's hunt flowers in the woods."

Heptha bothers the cook to prepare me special delights.

Anaktoria dresses up a song, Helen and Gyrinno dance, Atthis tries a musty joke.

It is a healing tempo...I am grateful...

These are lazy, summer days, the hammocks full, doves cooing in the olives. I send my thoughts on a long trip: may they find Phaon and bring him back to me.

This is theatre season and the talk is of actors and acting. I like to familiarize myself with a play before attending its performance because I can appreciate it much more. I never miss a play if I can help it, whether comedy or tragedy, though I prefer comedy. But I think the "offstage" is interesting, too—that is, if one can remain a spectator there. It is when we become involved that we lose our theatre perspective.

Neglates, who used to be a leading actor in Athens, likes to sit with me. He is our best critic. He is always urging me to write a play, "something about us," he says.

"The theatre needs you. Why don't you try? We need new blood."

I suppose he is right. If we rely on the old writers altogether, the stage will become stale. Perhaps I can think of something for the religious festivals next year.

Theatre means meeting people I seldom see anywhere else. I like the contacts.

People feel sorry for Scandia because he is the father of such a charming, marriageable daughter. White-faced, pinch-eyed, his neck twisted by a boyhood accident, one arm dangling—would they feel less sorry for him, if his daughter were ugly?

Andros is the next thing to a dwarf in size. He has the face of a twenty-year-old, although he must be well over fifty. He needs no one's pity—only some money! He is the best mask-maker our theatre has ever had.

Moonlight: Hand in hand,
Sappho and her daughter, Kleis,
walk along a path through hillside
olive groves, the ocean white below,
the murmur of waves part of their leisure and
sad conversation about Aesop.

y heart is heavy...Aesop, my friend, is dead.

He could have had a kinder messenger—it was Pittakos who brought me the news.

"The mob killed him for causing trouble in Adelphi," he said, his eyes cruelly cold. He had met me on the street, after a performance of "The Martyrs."

Did he think this the right time to let me know? Was it a warning?

I stared at him, as he shambled beside me. Then, before my face could reveal too much, I lowered my veil and walked away, trembling, my eyes unseeing.

I did not go home for a long time. I walked by the shore until the ball of fire sank wearily into the dark water. The hills had a beaten look, the sea an oppressive flatness. A gull's cry wept in me. Alone...alone... I was much more alone.

Alone in my library, I opened the box Aesop had given me and removed his fox, lion, donkey, raven and frog. He had moulded them for me. Two were made of light-colored clay, others of dark. They were as highly glazed as scarabs. I arranged them on a shelf above my desk and could feel my friend's presence, as though he were beside me.

But there would be no more letters.

No visit!

Lighting my lamp, I began my ode to "The Friend of Man."

I knew Alcaeus would be as disturbed as I.

I expected him to roar, "The mob!" Instead, he bowed his head, his hands on his lap, and remained silent. Slowly, he clenched his fists and gouged them into his thighs. Muscles corded his arms and swelled as he stood.

"He should have come here, to us!"

"He was sick, Alcaeus."

"Then I should have gone to him! Why was I doubly blind? I knew he was under attack for opposing the aristocrats."

Round and round, back and forth, we talked: what might have been, what should have been:

"If he had gone to Athens, he would have been safe with Solon."

"If only he could have stayed in Corinth..."

And remembering what a friend Aesop had been to us, he said:

"He knew I liked bread from that oven of Stexos... He was always bringing me my favorite wine."

"He couldn't do enough, that time I got so sick. The best doctors, he..."

"Wild boar, to help you get strong."

We recounted the fables, their Persian origin, the circumstances of their telling. How he loved travelers, especially from the East.

I see Aesop on his balcony, the wind making him blink his eyes; he has on dark blue trousers, yellow sash and gold blouse and carries his doll and is smiling and nodding.

Was it his profound understanding of life that made such a difference? He showed breadth of mind at all times. Revealing human character through animal traits, he taught us the comedy of our faults and aspirations.

Alcaeus has begun writing letters, to protest against this outrage in Adelphi, to alert friends, to cry out.

High on a hill, I sit and stare at my bare feet and try to guess how many steps they have taken.

I peer at my legs and consider the color and texture of my skin. I rub my hands over my knees and ankles.

What of Phaon's feet, the rigging they have climbed and the decks they have walked?

Storms have crashed over him. He has held his ship to sun and stars, legs spread wide, feet on the planking.

Does the sea mean so much to him? Is it his woman?

As I watch the arrival of boats in the bay, the unloading at the dock, I keep remembering his brown face.

The rains have begun.

They flood across the mosaic floor of the courtyard, draining noisily.

I am weaving a scarf, very white, light in weight, my seat a strip of rawhide on four pegs.

Around me the girls sit and chatter. Heptha and Myra weave together, working at one loom, whispering. The rain and wind come together over the house. Laughing secretly, Atthis and Gyrinno dash off, padding through the rain, across the court.

Kleis unwinds my ball of thread and keeps paying it out slowly, rhythmically, her hands in time to a song she is humming to herself.

The white wool is restful. I can weave nothingness or I can weave in my whole past, the sea, my house, the cliffs, the trees.

My fingers are Phaon's.

I have not changed my mother's house since she died because change is no friend of mine. Occasionally, I have had to repair or refinish a table, and a chair or picture, but were mama to return tomorrow she would feel at home.

I often think that I will meet her, as I go from one room to another, mama gliding softly, smiling, holding out her warm hands to me...we would sit and weave by the window, the sea beyond, our voices low. With our terra-cotta lamps gleaming, we would talk until late, too sleepy to chat any longer.

I can't remember my father, he died so young. His lineage, extending to Agamemnon, frightens me: That inheritance must carry into these thick walls and the glazed tiles—a strong house.

Mama gave me his royal flute, said to be carved from a bull's leg, but it has been years since I have taken it from its silk-lined box. Its sickly color never pleased me.

Its music comes to me sometimes: mountain vagaries, war music, sea songs, fragments of a day I can never know.

A bat coasts through my open windows.

Is there a better hour than dusk?

I feel that life is infinitely precious at such an hour, that sordidness and decay are lies. It is the hour when we cross the threshold of starlight.

Sometimes, before dropping asleep, I long to see Olympus, as part of this general dream:

Never is it swept by the winds nor touched by snow,
a purer air surrounds it, a white clarity envelops it,
and the gods there taste of happiness that lasts forever...

It has been a dreadful ordeal. I can hardly describe the events of this past fortnight.

I had barely recovered from the shock of Aesop's death, when word came that Alcaeus had been attacked.

I had gone to a friend's home and we had been chatting on the sea-terrace, when children burst in with the alarming news. I hurried with them to Alcaeus, the boys distressing me with their fantasies.

I found Alcaeus in bed, severely bruised and cut, with Thasos in attendance.

"It was Charaxos," Thasos said, quietly.

I must have gasped. I could not speak.

"I was alone...wandering," Alcaeus explained, then turned his face to the wall.

And I dared to hope that Charaxos would come to his senses! I pressed my lips to Alcaeus' hand.

"I'll get Libus," I said.

"Someone has already gone for him," said Thasos.

Libus, too, was shocked: he ordered the servants to bring Theodorus, another doctor.

As the news spread through town, people gathered in the street in front of Alcaeus' house, angry townsmen, yelling about Charaxos, calling on Pittakos for justice.

During the night, a mob threatened Charaxos' home, and in the morning, they stoned the place, battering shutters, screaming and demanding justice.

Pittakos sent soldiers to maintain order but the soldiers sided with the mob, forcing the doors, smashing furniture and chasing away the servants.

Sometime during the day, Charaxos and Rhodopis fled in one of their wine boats, heading for the mainland. I understand there was a fracas in the square, some wanting to overtake the ship.

For two days, I did not leave Alcaeus' home, taking turns at his side. In that circle of close friends, death pushed us hard, trying to break through.

Finally, Libus, more lean-faced and pallid than usual, from his sleepless nights and responsibility, drew me aside:

"He's going to pull through. You can go home and rest. Trust me..."

I slept and dreamed and came back and the days went like that before Alcaeus was out of danger, and we cheered him on the road to recovery.

Pittakos and some of his officials visited him, expressing their regrets, saying a committee had called, demanding Charaxos' punishment. I kept out of the room, leaving Alcaeus and Libus to handle the situation.

"Our tyrant sides with me!" Alcaeus chortled after they had gone. "I've won!"

It is a poor victory: we have not won back our years of exile. But, for the citizenry, this is something on the side of justice and worth talking about.

For my part, I suspect that Charaxos will return presently, unmolested. He is too important to our local welfare, employing too many, to be brushed aside. When his boat anchors, Pittakos will fine him lightly. By then, sentiment will have cooled.

Justice is rightly placed among the stars.

On my next visit to Alcaeus, I took my clay animals and placed them in his hands, describing each, one by one. He felt them carefully—too slowly—a sad expression on his face.

"So Aesop made them?" he said. "It's good you have them...proof that his world is still here. I wish I could remember his...his faith..."

Taking the figures from Alcaeus, I put them on a table between us: we three had sat at a table like this, in exile, planning, planning: those worries swept back again, distorted. Confused, I could feel myself trapped. I knew that in those eyes opposite me, death sat there, at least a part of death, the same death that was in those clay animals.

Our hands met across the table.

Villa Poseidon

It is useless to cross-examine Alcaeus. He will not discuss Charaxos.

"Here, do me a favor, read me something from Hesiod," he says, and hands me the poet's advice to his brother.

How history repeats itself! Family problems haven't changed: this is an earlier Charaxos, who bribed judges to deprive Hesiod of his inheritance.

If I did not know better, I could almost believe Charaxos had used this story for his model.

As time goes on, I feel the stigma of our relationship more and more. How can I be his sister?

Despite the liberality of our views, I am astonished that Alcaeus respects and trusts me. I can't shake my guilt: the fact that Charaxos has cheated and betrayed me does not exonerate me of blame. I am tired of all this. It is a confusion I can't accept indefinitely.

Phaon's ship has anchored in the harbor.

I have remained in my room throughout the day.

I have enjoyed the detail from my fresco—Etruscan girl strewing flowers, hair streaming over her shoulders, face filled with joy, arms outspread.

I am like that girl.

I took Exekias. As oldest member of my household, I feel she is the best chaperone. In her crumpled face there is more than Assyrian placidity: she has known me longest and is sympathetic and discreet: she says things the way my mother said them, so warmly I can't forget.

We left the house early, our scarves about our heads, women sweeping doorways and steps, sprinkling the dusty street, cleaning where horses and cattle had passed. Birds sickled from the eaves, dogs and horses drank at a watering trough, nuzzling moss, rubbing gnats, their hairy comradeship obvious in roll of eyes.

We had not been in the market long when I saw him, alongside a stall with a sailor, both drinking coconuts, shaking them, holding them up, tipping them, draining the juice, laughing. They had on shorts and were brown, incredible ocean brown.

Then Phaon saw me. Hurriedly, he set down the coconut and left the stall and came toward me, smiling, wiping his fingers on his shorts. In the way he spoke, in the way he stood, I sensed how he had missed me, other tell-tales in his voice and hands. And I knew, as we talked, that he sensed my longing as well: it brought us closer that we made no secret of our feelings.

A parrot jabbered atop its cage and a monkey squealed and battered at its bronze ring, until its owner brought bananas. People crowded us, elbowing with baskets of fruit and shrimp. Phaon and I walked under palm-ceilinged aisles, dust sifting around us, light finning through stalls, over herbs, nuts, wines and cheeses...the smells made me hungry. Together we ate Cappian cheese, tangy to tongue and nose.

"It never tasted better out at sea," he said.

"I hope everything tastes better now."

"It does...yes, I'm home again!"

Exekias ghosted behind me, face alert, her hands pushing me along; so we moved, past the pottery lads, one of them glazing a bowl between his calloused knees, the color as bright as the sliced oranges beside him ready for eating.

"Do you suppose you and I can sail again?" he asked, as we watched, seeing ourselves instead of the pottery boys. "There should be time...soon...when I'm unloaded."

I caught his half question, half statement.

"If I were invited, I'd consider."

My teasing brought a flash from him and laughter and he moved back a little, nodding agreeably.

As I walked home, I felt that my mind had been invaded by everything around me. I tried to hurry, thinking I'd remember all, the prices of the traders, the baskets of starfish, the white parrot; I'll remember his voice, his feet in the dust, his smiles.

Exekias babbled dully about food and flagrant cheating, her basket bumping my hip. I wondered how I could wait, through the days ahead, how could I occupy myself, until Phaon and I sailed? It was a question for water clocks and gulls, spindrift and wind, thought unfolding in my room, scudding across the floor to the window, stopping there, leaping out, to other lands, other times, backlashing with the net that contains yesterday...flames in a cruse...Atthis, slipping her perfumed hands over my eyes...

My lips burn, my hands are moist, I feel faint... Is that my voice, the sound of my laughter? Am I walking over these tiles?

Did I have supper last night? Drink? Rehearse a song?

My girls realize I am lost—wandering. I can't look into their eyes for long. When I see Kleis cross the room a trickle of ice slips down my back.

What if he finds me too old, what if my love doesn't please him...if he mocks me, or stands in awe, or wants to amuse himself?

Phaon...

I see you against every wall, against the sky, in the dark, in the sun under the trees. My flesh aches, my arms melt. Never has passion fermented so strongly in me.

Yet no messenger comes.

I can't bear the nights, to lie alone, to feel my breath on my pillow, feel the cool sheet.

In the morning, I ask Exekias questions, just to hear her voice, not listening, for how can she know whether he has forgotten me or is afraid or sick?

He is busy with his boat and port affairs. He has gone to visit his sister, with no thought of returning soon. He has sailed. He talks with his men—coarse talks. He eats, drinks, works, sleeps, snores.

No—he is fixing our boat for our trip.

No, he has many sweethearts, dark, tall, frivolous, lusty, daring—all young.

Why do I punish myself?

I hurt with weariness and desire. I will simply face the bedroom wall and shut out the light. No, I will concentrate on my work. What shall I write about?

Where is the sea that we sailed?

Was it a long trip?

Was our sail grey or brown?

Was the water rough?

The answers mean so little. Born of the sea, where is love more beautiful than on the sea? Like water, light, warm, swaying, the indispensable ingredient, the transformations, the necessities, the luxury, with the whites of the waves whiter than salt, with gulls flashing in the sun, with the bow of the boat swinging.

We swam, dove, played, laughed. There was bread soaked in honey and nuts dipped in wine and fruit, whose peelings we tossed to the birds. There was the creaking of the sail for our silences, the long brown tiller arm reaching to the sun, his hands on my shoulders.

He padded the bottom of the boat and we lay there, the wind heeling us briefly, the water sucking and his mouth sucking mine and the hunger of his body—the hunger I knew no sea could satisfy. Cradled, we talked softly:

"Was your trip good?"

"We had good weather for several days, then storms... It's like that, you know, most every trip. I try to keep far away from the coast, to avoid shifting winds. I keep farther away than most sailors. It shortens the trip..."

"You're not afraid?"

"No."

"When will you be leaving?"

"I have no cargo."

"Stay...Phaon..."

We had supper and I hated the food that kept us from our love-making.

A sponge lay on the floor and he dipped water over me as the sun washed over us, sinking rapidly. Why couldn't it stay for us? I saw him as Cretan, as Babylonian, as Persian, inventing his lineage. His atavistic hands moved certainly, oarsman's hands, netman's hands, the sea's...mine.

Nothing's more rhythmic than love with waves for bed, rocking, sucking, soothing. I lay there in his arms, thinking of the plants below, the glassy window of the water, the fish, coral, ruined cities...the lovers of other days, the mother of us all, love, pulsing in the rigging, in the pull of his legs, the hasp of his fingers. The rollers were kind to us, never too violent yet tingling the blood. The backs of waves looked at us. The spray spilled salt on our skin, gulls screaming.

We made love again, better than before, this time under the moon, our bodies wet from swimming, the summer night blowing over us, bringing us closer to shore where the surf boomed. Moonlight ignited inside the water and phosphorescence added to the brilliance. Flying fish sprang free. His body was so dark, mine so white...la, the rough of him!

Were any other lovers as happy that day?

As we stretched side by side, he said, with sleepy tongue:

"I remember an evening like this, a night of phosphorescence. I was lying on the deck, almost asleep. A flash tore the sky, silver light...it came streaking nearer and nearer. I woke some of my sailors. My helmsman shouted. We pointed and argued. The light hit the water and sent up boiling steam. We smelled something. Stripping, I swam where the light had hit the water. We were becalmed and I thought I had seen something white but found only dead fish, their bellies shining. The largest one filled my arms and I swam back to the boat and hauled it aboard. It had a brand across one side. We argued, and threw it back."

"What was it that fell?" I asked.

"Some said it was a star," he said.

"I was born in Pyrgos," Phaon tells me, his head on my lap. "I was born in a terrible thunderstorm, in my father's hut. He was a very clever fisherman but there were times when we got very hungry and on one of those times we waded out to sea, he and I, to throw a net...we were hungry. I wasn't helping much but I was there, small, perhaps learning something. Ah, that little island was barren and poor. And there I was in the water, the sun coming out of the sea, blinding me. And then my father screamed and I saw him fall. I tried to reach him. I splashed. I ran. I fell. I shouted. We were alone, we two. My father was thrashing about. It seems he had fallen into a pool, a rock pool, you know what they are. Maybe he forgot it was there, or didn't know. I can't say. But he had been hit by a shark and was bleeding. So I helped him, as best I could, both of us splashing, falling, the surf rising around us, big. He fell on the beach and I ran for help but before I could find help and come to him he had bled to death, on the sand, his hands on his wound, the wound from the shark."

We went up the mountain, to the outcrop and the temple, spent all day alone, the sheep tinkling their bells, the heat steady. He knew of a spring unknown to me and a hollow olive where bees had a hive. Only deep in the olive grove was it cooler and we buried ourselves under the trees.

The watery brown of his body was mine. I found his voice deeper than I had thought. I found his mouth. Discoveries went on, nothing repetitive, the wind, no, the olive shade, or the moss and mushrooms. Crushing a mushroom he rubbed it against his thighs. The smell of mushroom in the cool, dark place! His smell and mine; the smell of earth: life was a vortex of fragrances, peace on the fringes, then a shepherd's bell!

"I've wanted to be a shepherd," I said.

"It would be too lonely for me," he said. "It's lonely enough at sea. I look for a sign of land, a strip of floating bark, land bird or turtle. I look...there at the bow I'm always looking...now it will be you, ahead, in the sea. At sea I have my crew...no, I couldn't be a shepherd. But you?"

"For me, I'd have more time to think, to write, to gather the world of stillness. I could weave it into a pattern we'd recognize as important: succor, inspiration, hope. There is a cliff...you know it... the Leucadian cliff... I'd go there with my flock and dream as they fed about me, the sea below us, the murmur of antiquity around us.

It wasn't easy to visit Alcaeus and hear him talk, as he reclined at supper, his hands close to a lighted lamp, restless fingers, perturbed in a blunted way: the tensility of the battlefield gone from them: moving, they move in on themselves.

"Sometimes, I want to see a face...your face, Sappho. I want to see many faces, the faces of my men. I'd like to see a helmet and plume, the scarlet horsehair plume...color...what a great thing...

"My house has no window or door. Who wants a house that way?

"What of other blind men and their darkness! What good can that darkness do them?

"When my father was small he was scared of the dark. I never was. But this dark has become fear...words can't break it. Only sleep breaks it. When I'm lying in bed, on the verge of waking, I think, remembering the old light, I think, the sun's up. But where's the sun!"

Someone had dusted his shields and spears on the wall: I noticed the black point of an Egyptian lance, the cold grey pennons on a Persian hide: perhaps they had decorated the sand outside his tent.

This contrast troubled me and yet I longed to share my happiness: the child in me wanted to discountenance reason: the brown shoulders and rolling sea never left me as we talked and I tried to comfort, reminding him of days when it was fun to climb the hills and explore the beaches, fun all day: he admitted there had been time without pain and wondered why we were eventually cheated?

Fog leaned against the house and I described it and he asked me to walk with him. As we followed the shore, he talked of warriors he had know, "strategists," he called them; he boomed his words, excited by memories and the walk and the fog, which he could feel on his face and hands. His cane cracked against driftwood and I restrained him, to find his hands trembling.

The blue of the Aegean is reflected
in the faces of the 50 rowers of the trireme
as they chant and pull;
the blue is reflected on the ship's hull
 and the banks of oars.

*P*haon and I were offshore in his rowboat, the small sail furled, the surf near by, doubling into smooth green, sunset brazing the horizon. We had been gay, drifting, oar dragging, taking chances with the surf. Upright at the stern, Phaon looked about idly: we had been talking about going for a swim. Suddenly, he faced me and shouted:

"Over there...see them...pirate boats!"

"What?"

"Over there, the other way...those three boats...see the red shields at the bow...Turkish pirates...they're attacking Mytilene. I'll row for the beach. Hang on."

His oar splashed and the boat pitched; pulling with all his strength, he drove us toward the shore, the surf rising, the bow high. I thought we would capsize but before I could make out the pirate ships he beached us and we scrambled ashore, drenched and shoeless. Together, we raced for the square, shouting at everyone we met. Together, we dashed for Alcaeus' house, and threw open his door.

Men in gold, red and blue uniforms stormed our dock and invaded the town. I hung on, behind shutters, unable to tear myself away as the armed gang rushed past the house, forty or more, most of them yelling, one of them, in silver turban, whistling through his fingers, brandishing a scimitar. My mother had described such an attack...I could hear her and see her pained face...a terrible story I had never quite believed.

Phaon yanked shields and spears off the wall and armed Thasos and another man I scarcely knew, a visitor. Women and children hollered and scuttled inside, making for the rear of the house. Something crashed against our street door and men bellowed wildly at us. I saw wood rip the door. Thasos moved in front of me, urging me to hide. Phaon, with shield and sword, his clothes still sopping, threw open the door and beat off a Turkish spear. Catching two men by surprise, he wounded one in the neck and both fled, the uninjured man, a youngster, helping the other one, his shoulder turning red, their short swords rapping their legs as they ran. The injured man lost his turban as they rounded a corner...

"What happened...What's going on?" bellowed Alcaeus, behind Thasos.

"Turks," Phaon shouted, checking the damage to the door, swinging it on its hinges, his hairy shield high on his arm.

Long after dusk, men scouted the streets, all the Turkish boats at sea: the town buzzed with shouts and whistles: a drum throbbed: the raiders had killed two and injured several and plundered a winery and mill, removing flour and filling goat skins with fresh water at several fountains. I piloted Alcaeus about for a while, until my girls discovered me and begged me home, dreading a repetition, though by now armed soldiers had set up guards.

Stars shone brilliantly.

The bay, mirror-smooth, seemed utterly innocent of piracy and death. It accused us of our own folly.

Alone in my room, I reviewed the raid, our floundering ashore, our dash to Alcaeus' house, the brilliant uniforms, wild faces, wild cries, Phaon at the door, Thasos wanting me to hide, children whimpering.

The drummers were signaling each other, the surf sullen, the wind rising.

In a room near me, someone was sobbing. Peace would not return to my house or Mytilene for a while: how long, I wondered? Peace, how frail it is, how carefully it must be protected.

I realized I should comfort my girls and not sit and watch the ocean. It was hard to go to them, harder still to listen to their fears and accusations. When they questioned me I felt that what I described had never happened or happened to someone else. Atthis, holding a puppy in her arms, said she wanted someone to protect her and burst into tears, realizing how unprotected she had been.

Why hadn't I come with Phaon? What if the Turks had climbed the hill?

"You forgot all about us, you just left us here! Oh, Sappho!"

Next day, with my house quieted, I had time to write:

Accomplishments require sacrifice of mind and body; for some, accomplishment will be slow as the sea eating sand. I prefer the swift attainment—it is most inspiring. Death, because it is an incessant threat, retards progress, inhibiting our will to succeed, seeping under us at unexpected moments.

Surely, if we are to conspire against death, if we are to get the most of life, we must be clever, relying on intuition and knowledge, to reach any goal. Surely, the most important element in life is the humane, the kindly, the uncorrupted, tying together little things into something worth while, that will have significance now and later.

Poseidon
641 B.C.

Then, what is love? Isn't it sharing a personality never encountered before? I think it is this kind of interchange and it is exploring someone's thinking, with and without words. With Phaon, it is sharing the sea, the oarsman's hands, the swimmer's legs, yarns on the beach in the firelight. With Alcaeus, it has been our friends, our families, our town, our writing, our exile—years of knowing each other. The differences between Phaon and Alcaeus are so many it would be foolish to try to list them. Comparison gets me nowhere.

I suspect that love is too subtle for any analysis: love is so subtle it escapes while we look. Being in love is rather like being someone else, laughing some-one's laughter, tasting someone's wine, dreaming someone's dreams. I feel that close to Phaon. Together, we share the fire, the fire that wakes us in the night, that flies into our eyes, the fire that makes my mouth tremble, that makes me laugh in my mirror, that makes me test my perfume bottles and sends my girls for new powder.

I steal to him—with dignity. I crush him to me, dignity gone. I lose, I gain. I cringe, I lunge. Phaon, you are my body, in me, wanting you, wanting... We are the wanters, haters of nights that keep us apart, haters of time.

Its roaring deafens me: I, I didn't hear you. I, I was wrapped in thought. I was making love...I was reliving the sea, I was in the boat. I was planning our next meeting...I was singing... Darling, I was saying.

Riding donkeys, Phaon and I set out across the island, to visit his sister, riding all day in slow stages, to reach her hut and sleep there. I thought we would never find it, but that was my thinking. Phaon led us through a jumble of hillside rocks, through little valleys, right to her door, a hut of rocks and straw, her shepherd's crook beside the door.

Kleis is so unlike my Kleis.

She seems able to speak without words, perhaps because words are not very useful to her since she lives alone. She nods and smiles, her smile serene. Small, dark, light-boned, she appears out of the past, no sister of Phaon, unrelated to our island. I had not expected her to be so unlike us. Using her particular mystery, she made us comfortable, made us feel at home, a gesture now and then, a word, some roasted seeds, another word, as we talked. Her delight in having us was obvious, coming from deep inside. She has wonderful wind-swept sight, from the rapture of lonely skies, her communions. She is priestess of self-contained youth. She shared her food and we shared things we had brought. Phaon talked of his sea trip, the Mytilene raid, his voice in accord with her quality.

As our relationship deepens, I am more and more aware of his quality. It is best seen in his slow, slow gesture. Or in a spontaneous grin ending in a chuckle. It is in his carriage—his calculating look. His qualities are older than mine, seasoned by the primordial: his speech is older, in vocabulary, accent, intonation.

Kleis and I sang after supper, the supper fire burning.

Her sheep were near us, muffled, shuffling contentedly.

Venus hung over us.

How unlike my Kleis, in her singing and her songs: her songs are songs mother knew: they made me tremble and I wanted to clasp her to me: Phaon had forgotten most of them but joined us sometimes. We sang of lovers and wanderers.

She, the daily wanderer, was less a wanderer than any of us: her natural resources were always at her spiritual command.

Kissing me good night, she said:

"I love you for coming."

Going back home, we poked along, talking and resting at likely places. We stopped in an orange grove to eat, water rippling by us in an irrigation ditch. Cross-legged we ate cheese and dates and drank wine Kleis had given us, the summer smells around us, flowers, so many kinds of flowers in this place. Lying beside me, Phaon told me more about his life:

"...We met a storm off the Egyptian coast, the wind rushing us, tearing our sail. I was at the rudder when the sail split. I ordered my men to huddle in the lee and mend the sail. How we shipped water. The bow crashed. All of us thought we'd go down but they kept on with the mending, folding the fabric, squeezing out the water, wiping rain and spray from their faces. I've never heard a fiercer wind, raging off starboard...

"When we had the sail mended I had someone take the rudder and helped hoist. A wave bowled us over. It was nearly dark and the rain slanted toward me. Out of the side of my eyes, I thought I saw something on the sea, a man, a tall man. I said nothing but worked hard: I couldn't talk or yell in that sea. Part way up the mast, I looked down. Nothing. In spite of wind and rain, we hung our sail and swung out of the troughs. Back at the rudder, I saw him, saw him moving, white, tall, through the whipped tops of the rollers."

Villa Poseidon
641 B.C.

My girls still carry on about the pirate raid.

Gyrinno found a short sword and brought it to me.

"Look, I showed it to Archidemus and he says it's from the Turks. Those are rubies on the hilt, he says. Feel them. See...see..."

Her fingers tremble with excitement.

Her breath catches:

"What if they'd broken into our house? It would have been awful. Aren't you proud of Phaon?"

The whole misadventure leaves me cold. I think of the burial of our dead. I see the blood rushing down the neck of the wounded man. There was blood on Phaon's sword. He and Alcaeus had bellowed over their victory. Victory?

I pushed away the pirate's sword, and said: "It would be better if there were no pirates."

Gyrinno is disgusted.

What is wrong with man? Is man's piratical weakness an instinct? Women don't go in for piracy. We know the value of living and appreciate life's perilousness. We give birth to kindness...each baby is kindness itself.

I have forbidden Gyrinno to keep the sword: she must get rid of it, give it away, throw it away, I don't care.

Rain, rain, rain.

The girls appreciate my happiness since a sense of grace envelops me.

We weave and the rain falls, so gently, our looms fronting the windows and sea. I am weaving a white scarf, quite blemishless.

Weaving has always been the most delightful pastime: I sit and weave and the wool goes in and out: I can see nothing in front of me or I can see my whole past, or tomorrow, or Phaon, the ocean, my house, the faces of my girls...

I work silently sometimes, planning, composing. The art of weaving thoughts must have begun with the loom. The rain falls, and weaves its sounds. Atthis and Anaktoria sit on either side of me, Anaktoria singing to herself. She is dressed in white and Atthis wears blue.

Across the sea a wedge of rain scuds, slowly approaching our island. Shepherds are in their huts. Seamen are ashore. It is a time for all to rest.

At the bridge in town where I had watched the migratory flight of herons, I met Alcaeus. He was perched on the rail, cane crossed over his legs, waiting for Thasos. Glad to see me, he pulled his beard, fragrant and carefully oiled. I found him cheerful. He talked about a Carthaginian ship, in harbor because of broken oars, after sideswiping another boat in a thick fog. As I listened his face altered: it was as if he were in pain or remembered something tragic. Interrupting my comment, he asked:

"What's he like? Is he tall, this Phaon?"

I described him, touching his arm to lessen his resentment.

"So...he's not the soldier type!"

"Must he be?"

"No...a sailor, then!"

"Alcaeus!"

"I know...I know...the changes that have overcome me. I know them better than you."

"And I know my changes."

"Must our friendship end?"

"Alcaeus, let's not go on like this. We understand each other."

"Yes…yes…of course. I apologize… I should have scorned the war. Why was I bellicose?

"I could have kept to my books. I understand it takes infinite time to probe, time to evaluate, time to mature. I have always wanted skill—like yours, working, as you work, through intuition and knowledge of the past. By probing I could have come closer to freedom."

"You have found your freedom," I said.

"Where?"

"Attacking Pittakos, and his sort."

"That's another kind."

"I realize that."

As we strolled home, Thasos with us, he kept thinking, elaborating. Something hurt in me. Wasn't I deluding him? Was there freedom? When he stumbled, I stumbled.

He had been my Phaon. I thought of his encouragement, years ago, when each of us was desperate. That encouragement, that will to help, buoyed me and, talking swiftly, I promised him help, promised closer friendship.

Standing at his door, leaning on his cane, eyelids closed, he recited something heroic and it was my turn to change: my expression must have altered as quickly as his: his sincerity was an answer to mine: I knew he could not see and yet hid my face in my arm. Walking on, I felt he was still in his doorway, trying to see me, trying to understand.

A boy, with a yo-yo, asked me to stop and watch him perform tricks:

"Sappho…I can make it do things," he cried, dangling his yo-yo over my sandal, climbing it up my robe.

Sparkling eyes laughed and I bent and kissed him.

Yesterday, Anaktoria and I walked to a vineyard above the bay, a yard of crumbling walls, twisted, neglected vines, where bees hummed and swallows flicked apricot bellies. It was unduly warm and we threw off our clothes and lay on old leaves, in the shadow of a wall, the waves grumbling behind the stones, coming up, as it were, through masonry and ground.

I noticed her hand in the grass. I noticed my own. It seemed another's hand. The grass altered its identity. I felt my naked knee, pressing a stone: it seemed another knee although I felt the stone. I thought: nature tries to claim us before we are aware, before we are willing to let her. Swift, she likes to confuse, preparatory to that eternal grasp of hers.

Crickets piped under the wall, asking for cooler weather. Abruptly, they stopped, perhaps to listen to Anaktoria's singing. She sang until I fell asleep, to wake and find her sleeping, hands cupped over her breasts, afraid the bees might sting them. The wall's shadow had lengthened and birds were quarreling. Summer's integrity stretched from vineyard to horizon.

I thought about the two of us, our fragility, neither of us marred: sometimes, when someone is loving me, I am especially glad I have an unblemished body: I know my lover will have something to remember.

The ring Libus gave her glistens on her little finger.

Deeper, deeper—our love goes deeper, taking us completely; the early lamps sputter out; the stars gleam in the windows; there is talk of leaving, another trip to sea. But we shake off impending loss with each other's hunger; he says, your perfume stays on me; I say, the smell of you stays on me. He says, come closer, farther under. I say, I can't, I'm stifled, I'm submerged. Oh, impetuous lips. The depth of having someone your own, the depth of being the heart for someone. Phaon...the name, the body, the breath on my neck, special ways, his weight underneath me, supporting me, the sea coming through the windows.

There is nothing better than love.

O Beauty, you know I love him because he is the way I want him to be, you know he is kind...care for him!

A man speaks before the Acropolis in the moonlight:
"Stranger, you have come to the most beautiful place on earth,
the land of swift horses, where the nightingale sings
its melodies among the sacred foliage,
sheltered from the sun's fire and the winter's cold.
Here Bacchus wanders with his nymphs, his divine maidens;
and under the heavenly dew forever flourishes the narcissus,
the crown of great goddesses..."

have not seen Phaon for days and I feel eaten by rust, the rust that consumes bronze. I feel myself flake between my own fingers. Nothing distracts me. I tell myself I have no right to such feelings; it is wrong: be aware of the beauty around you, I say.

I have always believed that those who live beside the ocean should know more about beauty than others. Their minds should be richer, their faces kinder, their stride freer. Rhythm should be their secret.

I know this is false but I must evoke beauty. I must capture the magnificence of the sea and use its power. I must trap changes and repetitions, the storm's core and summer's laziness. There is superiority in these things, to help us through life.

But, with Phaon away, few things come alive: I am seaweed after the gale. Husk, why trouble others? So, I sulk. Or, when my girls insist, I revive briefly.

When will the atavistic fingers come and when will I smell the cabin's wick and the nets? Oh, drown me, Egyptian lion, Etruscan charioteer, lunge and shield: yours is the tyranny.

Surely feminine love is kinder, less responsible, graced with evasions. Masculine love is a beginning, an intensity that goes on. Masculine love pushes into the future, asking roots, a thread of continuity.

. . .

Last night, Phaon took me among terra-cotta lamps, their wicks flaming coldly. Perspiration glowed on our bodies. A cat jumped on our bed and Phaon pushed it away: wind rustled: leaves shook: flames swayed: this was the love I had wanted and I accepted it and made it live: no little girl's love, mine was glorious, damning all loneliness, knowing he would be gone again.

A dried flying fish revolved on a string above Phaon's cabin door. His boat rose on a gradual swell, seemed unwilling to glide down.

"Let me sail with you when you sail next time," I said.

"How could I take care of you?"

"Right in this cabin."

"Would you sleep on the floor?"

"Why not?"

"What about food? Food goes bad...our cheese spoils...our meat...our water. Sometimes we can't land a fish."

A smile wrinkled his face, as he hulked against the cabin wall, his smile vaguely reassuring.

"What about the heat and cold?" he went on.

"I was hungry and cold in exile."

"That was...years ago."

The flying fish spun, and I thought about time. Had so many years lapsed? I said no more. He had silenced me effectively for I could not endure those prolonged trials and no doubt the sea voyage was impossible: luxury had softened me. The spinning fish would have horrified Atthis. And was I very different?

But we sailed along our coast, hugging it, unloading fruit, getting away from the windless heat of Mytilene, selling dates, lemons and limes. As we sailed in a faint wind, the crew sang. Lolling under an awning, I heard stories of catches at the deeps just beyond us, deeps where the water shimmered flatly, as if of rock. One crewman, not much bigger than a monkey, dove for shells while we crept through shallows. Pink shell in hand, treading a wave nakedly, he offered me his prize, as I leaned over the side. Kelp floated around him and tiny blue fish darted in and out, under his legs and arms, angel fish lower down, perhaps frightened.

While the monkey-man dove for shells, youngsters swam from small boats, hailing us, boarding us, some bringing fish as gifts. A blond, husky body, his shoulders thickly oiled, shared an orange with a girl who had his oval face and fair skin: twins, I thought, and went to the stern to talk to them, comparing their arms and legs, their features and hair. The flock of youngsters cluttering our desk found us amusing and laughed at us.

The twins talked about a wrecked ship, "from a strange land...you can see her at dawn, when the water's quiet...she has a sunken deck, a huge rudder turned by chains. A great red and gold beast is carved over the stern..."

As we shared our oranges, juice trickled between her breasts.

Someone shouted and there was more laughter, and, as if prearranged, the youngsters abandoned us, dove overboard and swam shoreward, splashing, calling, wishing us luck.

I wish I were that young, I told myself.

That night, heat lightning brushed the sky, forming kelp-shaped ropes of yellow. Huge clouds massed about a thin moon and Phaon prophesied rain.

My head on his lap, we drifted, watching, listening to a singer, invisible man at the bow. His words made me uneasy as he sang of lovers lost at sea. Our sail had enough wind to fill it and yet we appeared immobile.

I drew Phaon's face to mine and his mouth tasted of oranges.

Above us, behind us, his flying fish rocked.

The lightning played among the stars and wet the sail and our helmsman bent sleepily over the rudder: it was a night for love and when the cabin had cooled, Phaon and I sought each other: he placed an orange in my hand, the singing went on, the sea sobbed, the orange fell.

"Phaon?"

"What is it?"

Keep me, wait, go on, love me, don't...I wanted to say so much.

I caressed him, breathed him in, the sanctity, the favor, the graciousness, the ephemeral. I wandered through caves. I dove to the wreck of the red-gold ship. I...

Later, we divided the orange and its sweet dribbled over us and he pressed his mouth there and we laughed, thinking with body.

I woke to see the moon sink below the ocean, to see how beautiful he was, his ship and fish swaying as a fresh wind clattered the sail.

Noon found us back in Mytilene.

PHAON

He is god in my eyes...
my tongue is broken;
a thin flame runs under
my skin; seeing nothing,
hearing only my own ears
drumming, I drip with sweat;
trembling shakes my body
and I turn paler than
dry grass. At such times
death isn't far off.

Anaktoria's flesh seems almost transparent—a sensuous softness coming from inside. When my girls are dancing on the terrace or in the garden, I wonder who is most beautiful.

Kleis spins. Atthis bends, arms upflung. I see a grape-tinted breast, fragile ankles. Yellow hair flies over shoulders. Gyrinno's throat is perfect. Malva's thighs. Look, Atthis and Anaktoria are dancing together. For an instant, their lips meet.

Tiles are blue underfoot.

Our wonderful harpist, an old woman, watches with burning, lidless eyes, remembering her naked days, playing them back again.

Cypress are drenched with sun.

Winter has come and Alcaeus has changed.

Winter—Libus and Alcaeus sit in my cold room, waiting. They have been waiting a long time for me; they were here when I returned from my birthday trip.

Alcaeus' face is deeper lined: it has been lined for years but something has happened abruptly, pain has pinched the flesh into new, tiny, angry wrinkles.

Friends have reported that he is drinking again and yet this is more than drink because I realize it is inner debauchery: the eyes cannot confess: instead, the voice tells.

We huddle in our warm robes, the wind howling, and he says, in this new voice:

"What has kept you? We've been waiting a long time."

Libus says:

"We haven't forgotten."

"Or isn't this the day?" Alcaeus asks peevishly.

"Of course it's her day," Libus says.

Alcaeus chuckles.

When was it, I kissed that face, admiring its masculinity? His hands never trembled.

Wind shakes the house.

Mind travels to other days when we struggled in exile, when Alcaeus, badly dressed, kept us in food, stealing, conniving. Often there seemed no way to get by. I sat, waiting, blind to life. That sort of blindness was weakness on my part, or acceptance or hope. Listening, while we drank, I asked what hope he had? He was deriving some satisfaction from his relationship with Libus. There seemed nothing else. Little by little, he forgot why he had come to see me: happy birthday became grimaces, guffawing, vituperations over battles. He and Libus grew excited, enacting scenes with their hands, shuffling their feet.

"This is how I beat off his genitals..."

Alcaeus roared, hand on his beard.

"I beat open his helmet..."

Yes, the war...

And in my room, I found relief listening to the wind, remembering the boat's passage to Limnos, my friends there, the festival in the vineyard, flute and drum, carom of bodies, laughter: Was it Felerian who laughed that low pitched melodious laugh? Was it Marcus who hurled his spear through the target? I erased Alcaeus: so much of life demands voluntary forgetfulness!

My girls had clambered about me at the dock, detaining me. Why does their love soften me? So often there are petty squabbles but, at reunions, they dissolve: the moment becomes a moment of accord, making life worthier: Gyrinno insists on carrying my basket, another smooths my scarf, another offers flowers. Kisses. They buzz into a flurry of plans.

"Tomorrow, we'll go up the mountain..."

"Tomorrow, we'll..."

Ah-hah-who, ah hah-who, the quails cry, as night comes.

I light mama's lamp, so smooth to the fingers after all these years, like alabaster. The wick struggles into flame, as if reluctant to leave the past.

My Etruscan wall girl comes alive.

"Ah-hah-who."

I take off my chain and pearl cluster and lay them in their scented box, pausing, sensing, dreaming.

Perhaps Phaon will be back soon—unexpectedly. I could not remain longer in Limnos, thinking he might return—tonight. I long for his mouth, the jerk of his legs, his *obelisko's* tyranny.

Hunger—let me sleep tonight, tired after the voyage.

No sooner have I returned than I am upset. Life is constricted... I stand among Charaxos' Egyptian treasures, confronting him: a twisted, gilded serpent god sneers at me: fragments of gold leaf blink: mellow gold is underfoot: I sway, as I talk, my parasol clenched across my belly.

"Now, I know," I say to him.

"You know what?"

"That you schemed with Pittakos, to have me exiled, with Alcaeus."

"What?"

"After all these years I've found out. Stop lying. You tried to get our home, that's why you wanted me exiled. What a brother you've been! What a fool I've been!"

For once he shut his mouth.

"During the war years you made many trips, to sell your wines...refusing to help me financially...yours is a debt you won't pay...and you don't care. I've dedicated my life to writing...I live no lie. I work to make life significant.

"And now, why have I come? To quarrel? No, to tell you the truth. I've nothing more to say. I want you to know that I know. It's a satisfaction..."

I could have talked on, but I left, snapping open my parasol, clutching Ezekias' arm, walking swiftly, curbing my pulse, hearing a seagull, the wind icy at the corners of the town, dogs sleeping in the sun, carts passing.

I tried to believe something was settled, that life was worth more for having told the truth. Yet, I wanted to return to Charaxos, demand apologies and restitution, apologies for impertinent, biased criticisms, as if apology, like a brand, could stamp out wrong, as if there were restitution for my cheated years.

Somehow, as I walked, as Ezekias chattered, Aesop commiserated: his hunchback shoulders squared my shoulders: his doll had the dignity of a scepter to prod my spirit.

A tow-headed youth greeted us and I thought: I wish I could have a son. Yes, to give birth again. That glory cancels many defeats.

In Libus' house, I turned to him and said:

"I told Charaxos what you told me weeks ago."

"But I shouldn't have told you, Sappho."

"It was time I knew the truth."

"And now you have an enemy," he said.

"He has been my enemy all the time, Libus."

We sat on his veranda, an agnus-castus sheltering us from the wind. His boy brought us drinks.

"Are we better friends?" he asked.

"I trust you more."

Tree shadows moved across his mouth and chin.

"Trust is not always friendship. I shouldn't have informed. How shallow we are, the best of us. We bungle. Friendship, yours and mine, it's hard to measure, perhaps we shouldn't try: isn't it better left alone? Friendship, that's what we've had all these years...I overstepped propriety."

How pale Libus was, in his grey robe, shadows ridging the fabric, chalking his face, thickening his lips, greying his hair. His sandals moved nervously yet he never moved his hands: they remained weighted to his lap.

I ate supper there, lingering with the ancientness of his rooms, dark mosaics, the crowning of a king behind him, Libus' chair of white leather, the king in the mosaic studying his crown, his jewels flashing red, a hint of Corinth and a hint of Crete.

Remembering my shepherd visit, I wrote this:

EVENING STAR

Hesperus, you bring
Homeward all that
Dawn's light disperses,

Bring home sheep,
Bring home goats,
Bring children home
To their mothers.

What is it urges the mind to seek beauty? What is the challenge? Why go where there are no charts?

Beauty says it is a kind of love.

So, I make love, in my quiet room, the word symbolic of man, life's continuity, my paper taken from reeds and trees. I write of birth, love, marriage and death, sensing that the unrecorded is vaster than the recorded. I sense the stumbling: the past could be a gigantic storm, fog obliterating at moment of revelation, fog fumbling from man to man, saying come, saying stop. The past is a wave through which no swimmer passes. As surf it inundates, then vanishes. On windy nights, it moans at my window, beautiful and hideous. I struggle on.

I quote from my journal kept in exile:

> *For three days we have had little to eat, days of quarrels, bitterness and savagery.*
>
> *I gave myself to a merchant and he has returned the favor by feeding Alcaeus and me. We ate in the kitchen, glad to find considerate slaves. We can remain long enough to recover our strength, if not our hopes.*
>
> *How I long for home and my servants, fish as Exekias can prepare it, onions in Chian wine, olives from Patmos. It helps to list the good things. Surely they are not lost.*
>
> *How wretched to cheat myself to keep alive, to cheat the face, the mooning eyes, the stupid mouth, the odor of flagrancy, the disbelief...chattel, cringe, lie still, perform.*

Copying those lines I remembered things I have never recorded, our filthy clothes, windowless room, flies, thirst, sickness...Alcaeus in jail... I was fined...authorities jeered at us...no sympathy, no luck until Aesop, his fox, raven and rooster.

I never thought him brilliant but he was always entertaining, agreeable about the smallest problem. Nuances come to me, as he told of a turtle that ferried a small turtle and then, at the end of the pleasant ride, said:

"Little turtle, you must pay."

"How can I pay?" asked the little turtle.

"By doing me a favor."

"Well, what can I do?"

"Hump along the beach and snatch me a fly."

"I'll do my best," said the little turtle.

After humping and snapping till almost noon, the little turtle brought a fly to the big turtle. Finding the big fellow asleep, the little one had to cuff him.

"Here," said the turtle, between closed lips.

"Ah," exclaimed the big turtle, swallowing the fly, tasting it with care. "Umm, that's the first fly I ever ate! You see a little fellow like you can do things a big fellow can't."

During the night an earthquake woke me and I wandered through the bedrooms, to see about my girls. Atthis needed covering and as I arranged her covers she murmured, "Mama, mama." Before I could slip away, she grasped my hand.

"Are you homesick, darling?"

When I kissed her, I found her face wet with tears. "Why don't you go home for a few weeks?" I whispered. "You were calling your mama in your sleep. If you're homesick, you must go home. Let's talk about it tomorrow. Do you want me to sleep with you?"

So we cuddled together and almost at once she relaxed and, after a few endearments, slept with her head on my shoulder, her violet fragrance around me. I held her fingers a long time. Drowsily, I asked: where do we go...why can't we remain young...happy? The last thing I recalled was the sweetness of her perfume.

The earthquake had been forgotten.

Alcaeus sat on his leather stool, his dog at his feet, sunlight behind him; elbows on his knees, he said:

"...I prefer that hymn. There's really no finer. In spite of time it's full of force, spring's arrival, the brevity of summer, the dying year. It has the shepherd's power, the forest's—passion tamed and sanctified. Another one I like is...

The woods decay, the woods decay and fall...

Libus, sitting near Alcaeus, quoted his favorite, huddling in his robe, his face averted:

> *Alone, in sea-circled Delos, while round on beach and cove,*
> *before the piping sea wind the dark blue storm waves drove...*

"Why do you break off?" I asked.

He did not answer but said:

"They knew, those ancients, how to supplicate the lowliest...they preferred the virginal...snowy peaks...whispering groves...the hunting cry..."

Warming my feet on a warming stone, I said I preferred the golden hymn and repeated fragments...

> *Long are their ways of living, honey in their bread,*
> *and in their dances their footsteps twirl, twirling light...*

Fragment of talk:

"We can't marry, unless we have a child...you'll be twenty-three soon...it must be like that...my house is a house of women..."

I thought of those words as I passed Phaon's house, beyond the wharf, isolated. As I passed, waves climbed its base, licking at boulders. Its walls are thicker than most, cracked and mottled. I used to be afraid of that house as a girl and as I passed these thoughts brought back some of that apprehension. I glanced at the seaward balcony, tottering on wasted beams, painted years ago. Seagulls squatted on the flat roof, as they have day in and day out. There are five rooms underneath those tiles and his mother and uncle lived and died there, a harsh struggle in rooms of simple furnishings, coils of rope, nets, brass fittings and bronze anchors.

Phaon lives there with two men, their servants and a hanger-on. Kleis visits occasionally. A parrot, some say nearly two hundred years old, gabbles sayings and fills the sea-sopped silences.

Yes, his house troubles me—its darkness, its evocation of poverty and my own exile.

While I was ill, Libus cared for me, the mastery of his hands relieving pain. By my bed, talking soothing talk, he brought gradual relief, just as two years ago. His hands are more than hands, it seems. Magical masseur, he explores yet never gropes: his fingers, padded at the tips, press, release, wait. Our friendship, with all its confidences, in spite of differences, weathers the years and is stronger at such a time, under his mastery. As he obliterates pain, he blinks absently or smiles his pale smile, withdrawn yet assuring. He learned his art from a young Alexandrian, a man he met while studying in Athens, who spoke many desert languages.

"I'd like to see him again. I've learned something through my own experiments; we would share. Of course, he's a great man."

And when I asked Libus about my illness, he said:

"Too much work, too much rich food, too much concern. You haven't been using common sense."

I didn't care for this and said:

"I know from what Alcaeus says, you help him more than anyone. You can help me."

"I'm not able to help him all the time."

"You mean his drinking?"

He shrugged.

"Let's call it something else. He does nothing so much of the time. That's where the trouble lies. He's not thinking...doesn't care."

"He wouldn't let me in when I went last. Thasos had to turn me away."

"The great soldier...drunk."

"What can I do?"

"Try again, Sappho. You and I know what he is—and was. You used to understand him better than anyone. Now, well, I do what I can. He's growing worse...have you heard him bellow at me or Thasos, as if he were commanding officer? No doubt you have...and more..."

Libus' hands pushed and then, feather-weight, stroked upward, over and over, inducing me to breathe steadily: his hands brought warmth, my thinking became clearer. As he pressed, the weight on my heart lessened; as his fingers covered my stomach, rotating their tips, I felt bitter anguish might not come again.

Lecturing me, he cautioned me about food and advised less exercise: rest, let the days flow by.

So, I sail with my girls, lie in the sun, walk, poke along lazy trails, fuss in my garden. Winter is hard on me. Chills come, leaving my stomach knotted, my eyes afire.

Phaon has returned.

Phaon and Sappho kneel in a grove,
a cithara beside them:
age-old trees shade the lovers:
the age of a ruined temple is part of
the timelessness of the grove:
bronze Phaon and white Sappho,
dusk takes over their whispers,
their motions, the wind in the olives.

*U*nder the olive trees we faced each other, alone, the sun coloring the ground, patching yellow and brown. A butterfly circled, as if considering us. Tenderly, Phaon fitted his hands over my breasts and I held him in my arms; swaying, we kissed: we had not talked much and we knew talk could come later: his legs crowded mine: his hand undid my hair, spilling it over my shoulders: confirmation was in that undisturbed place and accord burned our mouths and throats. Encystment was the slipping down of robes, our knees touching, the feeling, self, and underneath self, the ground, our earth: yet we were not aware, only before and later: the consummation dragged at the trees: I forced him to me, forcing back his face, his mouth: how warm his stamina: tenderly, we rose, to fall back: tenderness, how it becomes ash, taking us by surprise: I couldn't stop quivering till his hands stopped me: his voice was real so all was real: then, he was home and this was not a lie: I knew it on the slope of hills sloping to the ocean: I knew it in the boat, far at sea.

When we learned of a terrible earthquake at Chios, we loaded Libus' boat with food, wine and water and set out, before dawn, across choppy water, Phaon and I at the stern, under blankets, Libus managing the sail. We were part of a small fleet but I couldn't discern another boat. Spray swished overhead and fog, ahead and astern, seemed ready to pincer us. Under our hull the water flooded ominously; the sky, without its stars, might have been the ocean.

Our hard trip brought us into Chios tired and hungry; we had been unable to look after ourselves but, without eating, we began to distribute food and wine.

Chios—happy town—lay broken. I walked about, remembering, stopping here and there: all the central part, shops and temple, were dismembered, had windy dust blowing across it, greyish dust that seemed mortuary. Yet, I saw no dead, only the injured: Libus helped them, bandaging, talking: I gave wine and water, afraid: he was annoyed by my fear: I could not find Phaon and that worried me. Wine, and water, dribbling them, my hamper shaking, the wind icy and dust in my mouth, I felt sick again. A child raced to me, wailing: crouching down, I mothered her, fed her a little bread: as we crouched, a slab of building fell, tottered forward and disappeared in a wave of dust.

"The quake came and came and then came again," an injured woman said, accepting dates and cheese.

By now, I saw others from Mytilene and their hearty faces cheered me. But how the gulls screamed. Flocks wheeled and screamed.

On the beach we lit fires and cooked our suppers, wind and dust still bothering us: Phaon and I ate with people from home, our fire put together from the prow of an old boat, the talk about Chios and the injured, their lack of food and care. We slept in beached boats, the surf snarling, stars breaking through fast clouds: I remembered the big dipper and frightened people... Libus woke us early and we did our best to help, using splints, caring for a head wound, bandaging a boy's chest... Libus scarcely allowed himself time to eat.

The wind had subsided, and I felt less fear and went about with my basket of food and wine. In the afternoon, we welcomed other boats from Lesbos and after a second night on the beach—this one calm, all the stars awake—we sailed for home, three of us leaving at the same time, our boats so many grey corks on a line.

As I stared back at the stricken town, I heard the gulls. "Phaon, it was bad," I said.

"Yes, very bad, though I've seen worse."

"I hope I never do."

"These people had help...sometimes there is nobody to help."

"We're in the lead," Libus cried. "We'll be the first ones home. Now for some sleep."

Today, I had a letter from Solon: he discussed politics and his immediate intentions and then went on to consider my poetry, praising it for its lyrical quality, refreshing themes, compassion and sense of beauty.

I respect his judgment and his quotations sent me to my books, to reconsider and evaluate. For a while, I sat at my desk, thinking over passages, contemplating the ocean, serenely blue as usual. Life, for the moment, was balanced: it had acquired profundity and calm: here was my reward since I believed his assessments just: for once, I needed no one to share: I needed nothing.

But I picked up Aesop's clay fox and recognized my need: the bite of yesterday cornered me.

Kleis has fallen in love—this time with a cousin of Pittakos. I am amused, and have done all I dare to make the pair happy, picnicking and boating.

I have seen him at play on the field, built well, long of leg, with a homely, genial face and grin that consistently makes up for mediocrity. Like his cousin, I could add. But that's unfair. When I see him screw up his mouth in front of Kleis, I sag. The next moment he brightens and seems about to say something intelligent. Then, the cycle resumes. Love, I remind myself, with inward nod, can be curious.

Well, I am playing the game—if it is a game—circumspectly, knowing winds can be fickle. I gather news from my girls who too often babble.

"See, how she conducts herself! She's grown up!"

"My, they're serious!"

I am aware of her airs.

Am I to forget her clandestine meetings of a few months ago and expect her golden head to settle down?

She confides in me and I conceal my smiles.

However, doubts from deep inside prompt me to accept and not go in for ridicule: where is another daughter, where is the boy suited to your taste? Is she to fall in love your way? Deeper, I discern the sacredness of life, elements of faith and love.

Thinking these things, I go where the hills plunge to the bay: I listen, under my parasol: there is much more than sound or silence: I am confronted by yesterday, in the gulls: I squint, and there, on milky horizon, I glimpse the spirit of man, blundering, a plant in his hand, a rope dragging behind him, a dog by his side: what is the rope for?

I think of my school and how taxing it is to teach kindness, moderation and beauty: yet, I am confident, teaching is worth while and living worth while: good meals, laughter, music, dancing, love: they are there with him and his dog and the rope, in sound or silence.

Kleis, may you find a good way, all the way.

For my part, my relationship with Phaon affords discovery, Sumerian lassitude, great rivers and forests, prowling sand, the bay and its currents, the hull dipping, the rower heaving his arms, groaning.

Illusion, deceit, whatever it is, this is the happiest period of my life.

As I walked by the columns of my garden, I recognized that never have I accomplished so much. I have unlocked doors. I see my esthetic way: my personal recollections have pulled out of ruts. I have uncovered uniqueness, sensibility... I have seen what it has cost man to survive: dunes against dunes, lack of water, perilous heat: I have weighed his potential, his grace, his beauty. I have sensed that appalling black that existed before the coming of books. I have heard torn sail and smashed rudder. I have felt the foundering.

That darkness must not come again!

We must see to that!

I walked among my statuary and benches, absorbing the difference in roses: home and happiness were secure in me: my writing must be a part of this place: marble benches, a face augustly seaward, lichened with green: another face turned toward the sun, his enigma personal, his serpent's head prowling through a disc.

I found this in my journal, written more than fifteen years ago:

> *Yesterday, Cercolas and I spent the day in an olive grove where men were knocking olives off the trees...we walked far.*

That is all I wrote and yet that was one of the most joyous days. What kept me from describing our happiness? Was I too close to it? Or was the next day one of those hurried days and I thought I would write about our day later on? Later?

A year later Cercolas was dead at war.

And what made those hours precious? It was our accord, the day itself and everything we saw and did. I realize this now. His arms were around me, or mine curled about his waist. His mouth went to mine, many times. Mine to his. I wish I could remember what we said but I remember his smiles and I remember his coarse brown Andrian robe and I remember how we looked at this and that, making each thing ours.

Cercolas...your name is euphonious...your fingers reach out of death...I glimpse your smile.

But is this all that remains when we are gone?
Is this the answer?

I have often relived the experience of giving birth. Had Cercolas lived, there would have been other children. Kleis was born on a summer's day, the ocean lapping after a windy night, a dragonfly in my room, clicking its wings over my bed. Mama saw it and murmured:

"There...see it above you. Now, I know you'll have a girl!"

Shortly afterward, Kleis was born, the dragonfly still there: how blurred, it seemed, and how the ocean faded and reappeared as I fought. I felt I would drown in sweat, drops pouring down my neck. Mama wiped my face and hands, her voice soothing, as she cooled me. I wasn't afraid: no, a new happiness surged through me, even while my wrists were breaking and my knees afire. Even while the pain tore me, I was aware of this happiness: I was bringing life, defeating death, adding to our world. My heart sang, though sweat drenched me, and the dragonfly, clicking its green wings, seemed a ragged dot or great bird.

I was glad Cercolas wasn't there: I tried to remember his love-making but all I could remember was pain and mother's voice and the chatter of Exekias and the sound of the sea. When Kleis had come, I thought: my wrists are broken and my knees burn but I'm glad, glad...and mother kissed me and said: Go to sleep, darling.

When I woke, the top of the ocean had become pink and pink webbed the sky: it seemed I was staring through woven stuff, skeins in rows, with wool dropped and tumbled between: the pink darkened nearest the water and stars were visible—a sunset like many others and yet different because Kleis was here: this was her first sunset.

During exile, when Alcaeus and I had the same room and bed, he tried to make me feel our bad luck couldn't last. He would roar against it. He might begin the bleakest day with a song.

"Hungry—let's go beg!

"Thirsty—let's find a fountain. There's cool water in the shade of a carob."

Our feet grew blistered. Days I lay on my mat, too sick to move, he brought me bread or a flower. Kneeling by me, smelling of the streets, he'd rub my hands...

"We'll find a way."

When we shared the big bed at Aesop's, its sides painted with flowers, Alcaeus cheered, reminding me of our luck.

"Remember those candle stubs I found?" he laughed. "Remember the roast lamb I stole—how the guy rushed after me, jabbing the air with a knife. Remember..."

I remember my gratitude to Alcaeus and Aesop must not end. Without their help I would have died.

I dreamed the other night that Alcaeus and I were exiled again, that Alcaeus came to me, as I lay between heaps of dung: he crawled toward me, clothes in rags, exhausted, blind. I opened my cloak and offered my breast—wanting to suckle him.

Waking, I realized how late it was.

Four of us, with Libus as guest, had supper at a table on the porch, a reception to honor Anaktoria's return...*bourekakia* and stuffed grape leaves, Anaktoria serving, maturer with that overnight bloom, that overnight assurance.

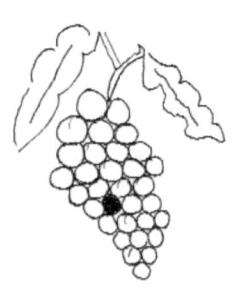

"Do you like *bourekakia?*" she asked Libus, too obviously thinking of him, offering him stuffed leaves instead of *bourekakia*, offering herself, at least for the night, something in that spirit, making fun of Telesippa, her newcomer rival, who was also interested in Libus, diverted, momentarily by someone's comment about my harp, a point to bandy for effect: how charming they were, bathed and perfumed, Telesippa in her city clothes, Anaktoria in her Cretan style, Gyrinno's jewels amusing us, the topaz swallowing her throat.

"You see Sappho's harp has twenty strings and is for Mixolydian songs."

The topaz tinkled and a smile went round, coaxing us to feel better.

I told them about the harp I had invented, admiring them as I talked, hair, shoulders, arms...enjoying each girl. I realized they were especially mine. No one else would have such an opportunity to influence them.

We listened while Anaktoria described her visit, her baby sister, the sailor who died on the wharf, the arrival of an Ethiopian girl, slave for a merchant. She talked as I had taught her, gestures well timed, head poised. She has lost her island mannerisms, such as gulping impulsively and biting off chunks of food.

Brushing aside her shoulder-length hair, blue eyes a little wild, Telesippa gossiped about her dressmaker, "the best in Athens," whose "tattling is incessant."

Libus steered the conversation to something sound and Atthis carried on: yes, no doubt, teaching helps.

Later, we sat on our terrace and passed around sweets and nuts and Libus joked, sultry jokes of the last generation, wanting to impress the girls.

Old tiles underfoot...youth around me...the thick walls of my house above the sea... I relaxed until someone mentioned Phaon and I saw him working on his boat, hands stained with oakum, knees rough from the planking.

"Phaon—I say good night to my girls. You'll be with me, soon. Soon, I'll be buried under your mouth."

Tomorrow, we meet after the games on the field.

I'll see him there, legs flashing, discus flying, his spear digging its hole. I'll see him rock with laughter and splash himself clean.

Alone, I rubbed my hands over my body, thighs, breasts, ankles, wrists and shoulders: my flesh is firm: I know, as I sense my own integrity, that before long I must lie in death.

No waking touch on my belly and knees, no chance to comb and dress my hair at leisure, no mirror for dawdling, no winging of gulls.

Poseidon

Of the poems I have written recently, I like these most:

> *Love, bittersweet, irrepressible,*
> *Loosens my legs and I tremble.*

.

I could not hope
To touch the sky
With my two arms...

.

The sun sprays the earth
With straight-falling flames...

.

O, Gongyla, my darling rose,
Put on your milkwhite gown...

.

When seastorms scream across the water,
The sailor, fearing these wild blasts,
Spills his cargo overboard...

.

The night closed their eyes,
And then night poured down
Black sleep upon their lids.

Alcaeus prefers the last two.

In a vase, on my table, a white rose opens and I see the face of Anaktoria. The rose is the most perfect flower, some say. Of the two kinds, the garden and the rambler, I prefer the rambler, climbing through the night, bringing its fragrance into my room, white in the starlight, ivory in the moonlight.

The sea and its waves are something we never forget yet never remember: how the surf leaps and splits into foam, how the foam cascades into white and divides into blue. From shore to sky there is blue, in patches like marble, areas like grey and porous granite, ribbons of blue that submerge in whorls.

How quiet the blue, how serene where afternoon sun polishes a path aimed for the shore, Cretan, Ethiopian, Etruscan, where men and ships have sailed— their hieroglyphs ruddered by chance. The ocean is always chance, yet it is subdued, finally modulated by place and time. Wherever we travel, there is the element of chance, rain, storm, heat, cold, before us, deceptive, feminine, wrapping us in fog, cities, deserts, islands, birds, starry decks and windless watches.

We never remember the sea because it alters momentarily, making rainbows, spreading colonies of butterflies, floating celery stalks, turtles, heaving shells and driftwood—beaching itself with footprints that fill with seepage or disappear underneath the wave.

Cercolas and I had such fun, when we were newly married and rode our white mares, across the island and along the shore, sometimes swimming them. When the oldest became sick, I put a pillow under her head and tended her until she died, on the beach, beneath the thatch of her stable.

Cercolas took the other mare, to die with him at war, I suppose it was. How can I know?

Our horses have gone, six or seven at a time, until there are only colts and old ones—I see them on deck and in holds, their white faces peering, yellow manes shining: white, in memory of our mares, white as gulls. I wish I could hear their whinnying across the fields, as they race toward me.

Warriors brag about their fearless horses but I prefer mares that nip my hands and tug my clothes.

Music is a tree, a cave with sea water sloshing, a shell to the ear, a baby's laughter, the lover's "yes." I suppose it came from the flint, the arrow. Cercolas was music. Mother was music. The loom and harp are music. I have heard music in my dreams. I dream many kinds of music when I play the harp.

I like music best at night, under the stars; I like it when I lie down in the afternoon, aware, yet not truly aware; I like it when I am up the mountain, the wind harsh; I like it when I am on the shore, the beach fire low, sparks rising, the sea almost at rest.

I like music when I eat, when I am at the theatre, or alone. Lonely music is marrow-wise, aware of secrets, revelatory in surprising ways, prying, blurring—

altogether deceitful. I like the harp better than the horns. Drums frighten. The voice is best: its story is man's, the sea's, the mountain's, and the sky's.

How I used to laugh at rimes Alcaeus wrote against Pittakos:

> *Old Pitt, we found your cloak*
> *Among the fish and fisherfolk;*
> *We saw your mouth gape and perk*
> *Whenever a blouse made something jerk.*

I suppose Pittakos paid many a visit to the fisherfolk—he was young enough then. And Alcaeus was clever enough to wring every drop of satire out of P's doings. His foolery endangered many of us. What a disgrace Pittakos remains in office. How fine it would be if Libus were empowered.

Libus says:

"There aren't enough of us to overthrow this man...he's entrenched till he dies. It's better to wait. Look at Alcaeus, what has his fight gotten him? Part of his tragedy comes from his inability to overthrow this man."

Yesterday, when I visited Alcaeus, I shivered and pulled back. Alcaeus stepped forward and grabbed my hand.

"Come, darling, we're having a drink. Join us."

Libus signaled me to sit down: their dining room was full of phantoms; shields glared; pennons dragged at me. With an apish grin, Alcaeus reeled across the room to bump against a table and chirp a drunken song.

It was rainy and dark and the melancholy afternoon and room closed in. You must pretend, I said to myself. Pretend he can see. Pretend there's nothing wrong...imagine...

As the three of us drank together, a scrawny, red-fleshed boy served us, downcast, looking as if recently beaten.

As we drank, the melancholy of Alcaeus' soul spread, seeping through taut throat muscles: intelligent things said with difficulty, good things said badly, reminiscences slightly distorted. What is more dismal than a damaged life, damaged beyond alteration, no matter how much we care? What more futile than communication at such a time?

I could not look at him but looked at Libus instead, his ephemeral face growing more ephemeral as he continued drinking, wrestling with his dogged silence.

Drink could not help... I fled home.

Mytilene
641

Three soldiers have been washed up on a raft, scarcely alive: all of them were taken to Alcaeus' house to recover, if that is possible. Libus wanted them there, to care for them. They are islanders and had been imprisoned over a year. For days they had been adrift, paddling, foodless except for fish and birds. I hear from Thasos that one of them, not much older than Phaon, throws himself against walls and stalks about babbling to himself, begging for water.

Alcaeus is in his element, determined to help these derelicts: he's captain again, in command: he's kinder and more resolute with this trio, which he believes he understands: oh, I sympathize with these sun-blackened wanderers, these lovers of freedom who defied jailers. I, too, know what it is to defy, and what it costs.

I sent them food but I could not go to them.

Later, I changed my mind; I wanted to see them, to see what their failure had done to them, what their fight had cost. I decided I might be able to encourage them, so I brought Atthis and we asked Libus to let us in and we talked to two of them, giving them food and helping them eat and drink, and everything went well till the mad fellow heard us and hurled himself against the bedroom door and burst in, to collapse in a heap, jabbering, writhing, eyes rolled back.

Atthis jumped from her chair and cried:

"Uh...how terrible...like a worm!"

Libus knelt by the young man and his hands quieted him. Not a word was said: then he turned to Atthis:

"He's been through a lot. Exposure...heat...no food... We can help him. He'll be all right, in time."

With a few reassuring words, he got the fellow up and led him away.

Later, I learned that one of the older men is a cousin of Phaon's. Phaon has heard the details of their days on the raft, and I am pleased by his kindness, the hours he gives to stay with the pair.

He and Libus are restoring them: food and encouragement are cancelling horror. Even the mad fellow is mending, eating and drinking normally, talking rationally much of the time. Phaon's cousin claims he fought with Alcaeus, but Alcaeus can't identify his bearded soldier: is it lapse of memory?

Or was it, as the cousin says, the period when Alcaeus lay injured, the spear wound in his skull healing, those weeks of pain that brought about his blindness?

Sappho and Phaon, in a small boat,
drift seaward, oars dragging:
shimmering light seems to tow the boat seaward.
Stripping, bronze, Phaon dives
expertly and brings Sappho a handsome conch:
listening to the shell they lie in the boat
and begin to make love,
a bronze gull sculptured on the sky,
the sound of waves.

haon's crew is loading his ship with pottery for Byzantium, a cargo that has to be delivered soon. This realization sharpens our love, though he thinks too little of distant voyages and I trouble him too much with warnings.

Summer is upon us and I accept the lethargy of eating, sleeping, dreaming. He likes summer heat, our damp bodies, my sticky perfume and sticky fingers... cool drinks. He enjoys fruit mixed with coconut and has had my girl prepare mixed salads...

"Fruit. In hot weather, nothing's so good. And there's never any fruit at sea."

"Not for long."

"You know...when I come back, Kleis may be married. Your family will be bigger, you know." He talked languidly, with his cheek against mine, as we sat on the beach.

"I hadn't thought of that."

The thought troubled me—fixing time around me: Kleis could not be this old!

Baskets and dishes cluttered the sand around us, wind puffing, light ebbing to lavender, fog on the water, floating above the surface, a boat creeping, its mast slicing misty layers, moving between floors.

What shall I give him for luck—a charm? A coin?

Why not my mother's drachma? She was lucky: there was no war in her time: she had lovers and then a husband to whom she was faithful. She did not have to endure an island without young men and know what it was to live among women for ten years.

Yes, the old initialed drachma of hers...

The loading of the amphorae was delayed and we sailed in his smaller boat, with a crew of three, to the bay where the wreck lies, our sailing so smooth the hem of my skirt hardly swayed. Phaon equipped us for diving and since the ocean lay incredibly calm, we located the wreck easily by tacking in circles. Kelp had snared the masts—giant legs of brown. Her masts struck fists against us, as greenish fish crossed and recrossed her deck. Splinters of light sank straws, fidgeting straws that reached the dragon's gold and red.

I worried, afraid of kelp and fish.

Phaon disappeared beyond our bow: his brown arms yanked at the kelp; he bobbed and swam toward me, treading water, puffing.

"Let me help you."

"No. It's too deep," I refused.

He and his crewmen dove by holding rocks meshed in pieces of net; they coaxed me until I had to try, sliding down rapidly, too fast for me: I knew I could let go of the rock or jerk the line attached to it and be towed upward; I wanted to be brave and gulped and oozed out bubbles, peering up. I wanted to put my feet on the wreck but I never reached her. Lungs bursting, I swam upward, soared, unable to see clearly. My lungs hurt a long time afterward, as I lay on deck, amazed at the crew's folly and strength: there was no end to their enthusiasm, their plunges from deck and rigging: by sunset, they had hacked through the wreck, entering the dead cabin: when we raised anchor and swung for shore I was glad, and hungry.

That night, I dreamed of gaping fish that carried coral fans: our sail became a net that filled with fish of reddish hue, then sank, to be towed to sea: all night a gentle sea rocked us, the dipper above our rocky shore.

In the morning, while the bay lay limpid, before I could finish eating, our men dove and chopped. As I lazed, birds spiraling, someone hollered and floundered toward our boat and I rushed to the side to see a sailor with a green cup, treading water, offering me his prize.

So the men had not been excited for nothing.

Phaon was as pleased as his men. Hunkered on the deck beside me, he nicked the green of the cup's rim and uncovered gold, the gold gleaming. I'll remember his hands as he passed the cup to me.

Who made it, how old is it, how long was it below? we asked each other, as I held the cup, our deck swaying.

The crew's crazy conjectures and laughter went on, as they went on diving.

It was hard for them to give up and sail for home: stars pegged our rigging and flipped over glassy combers: fish leaped: we watched as great white crests rose: we slept and woke, our deck slanting, boom groaning.

Phaon woke and we talked, of our separation and reunion.

"You will be gone a long time!"

"Perhaps my trip won't be so long."

"Let's come back to the old wreck."

"Will you dive?"

"I tried..."

We whispered and saw the dawn, a dawn that had streamers of rain splotching the horizon, pelicans one after the other in long files, our island in the offing, quite black.

I was sleepless most of the night, getting out of bed, restless because of the warmth, standing by my window, waiting for a breeze, the stars out, Mercury but no moon, the stars and the crickets and a nightingale and the sea, and someone, somewhere in the house, moving, then silence. I was thinking of him, wanting him, and I began a poem, changed it, rephrased it, thinking, my body needing his body:

> *Slick with slime to satiety he shoots forward*
> *playing such music upon those strings,*
> *wearing a phallus of leather,*
> *such a thing as this enviously,*
> *twirls, quivering masterfully,*
> *and has for odor the hollow mysteries,*
> *orgies for leaving, orgies for coming;*
> *the oracle comes, comes with companions,*
> *comes with mysteries, lover of mine,*
> *displays this randy madness I joyfully proclaim.*

I started the poem once more...such a thing as this enviously, that's suitable... twirls, quivering masterfully...hollow mysteries...there are good things...

Dawn came and there were the sounds of pigeons, gulls, servants coming and going, girls whispering...the laughter of girls.

The bay lay almost black and Phaon's ship was quiet, its mahogany rails shining, someone leaning over, utterly motionless. I looked about for a moving bird or a boat. Huddled on the wharf near me, a man slept, toothless mouth open, nets over his legs and thighs. A similar mesh covered the water, as far as I could see.

Wanting to say good-bye, I stood to one side beside Atthis and Gyrinno, chilled, afraid. The slow unwrapping of the clouds irked me: a number of men arrived and carried bundles aboard, their motions slow, their laughter irritating. Was man always oblivious?

Then, from at sea, voices came, shifting uneasily, an oar creaking between unintelligible words, a dog whining, a girl coughing. Loneliness filtered from the sky and depths.

The man still leaned over the rail...

"Off with the ropes."

"Everyone's aboard."

"Let's sail."

It was Phaon's voice: "let's sail": and he called to me, called to all of us: I heard Libus and Alcaeus: I heard the oars: as the ship headed seaward, Atthis hugged me and my loss was in that receding figure at the stern, sail climbing the mast behind him: had I shouted good-bye?

Bitterness struck me: again I knew I had no right to such a mood. Better to have a fling at Charaxos, there on the wharf, in his white clothes, sullen, bellicose, his friends snubbing me as we walked past.

Home seemed meaningless.

Had Alcaeus felt this way, on his return?

I knew he had and knew he had had ample reason and threw back my head, as I opened my door, and walked to my room alone, determined to think clearly: but it was no more than a resolve and the loneliness of those sea voices came and that voice, saying: "Let's sail."

My ocean window called me.

Was that his ship, that mere dot, that point of wood under banks of cloud?

I couldn't keep back my tears: what was it, his spirit, his dignity, his thoroughbred body? No, it was the conjunction of these and the very thought, this summary, increased my sense of loss. He was warmth, impulse, reason for living. Words! And he was more than words!

By now the dot had disappeared and against the clouds, birds wheeled and drifted and scattered raindrops fell, scenting the air. I went out and let them wet my face and take away the sting and then closed the shutters of my room and lay down.

Rain has such music.

I let it lull me to sleep, sleep, in the morning, warm, in my bed, a day or a year...sleep...was it from the depth of the sea?

That night a storm engulfed us, ransacking our trees, banging our shutters, moaning over the roof until Atthis got into bed with me, thoroughly scared.

"Don't be afraid, darling."

"I am...I am...Aren't you?"

"No...maybe a little."

"What about Phaon?"

"He's far at sea by this time."

"But isn't that bad, to be far at sea?"

"I don't know...hush."

I resented her pliant body and scented arms and hair: yes, at sea, Phaon must be battling gigantic combers: his cargo might shift...his sail might... When Atthis hugged me, I felt stifled and yet, as she quieted and the storm continued, I was grateful I could comfort her. If I could not have Phaon, I, at least, had someone who loved and needed me.

Rain and wind knocked open the shutters and I rose and closed them and dried my feet and got into bed again.

Floor tiles had chilled me.

Rain cuffed roof and sides of the house... I heard the surf growing wilder, sloshing over rocks, climbing the lower cliffs, rising and falling onto itself with a hiss.

I straightened my hair on my pillow, knowing I had hours to wait: I said, you've seen a lot of storms, sleep. Your island isn't in danger. But, nothing could keep me from thinking of his boat and its struggle. I named off members of his crew. I named their families.

Phaon's cousin was with him—a wretched re-initiation, after those hideous days on the raft.

I heard Anaktoria and Gyrinno talking in the next room.

I thought of the madman, living with Alcaeus, walking about with him: I'll make something of him, Alcaeus had said to me, the face revealing that his madness had not left him.

> *Joy and exaltation are the triumphs...*
> *today is the imminence...*
> *even shadows have their fire...*
> *the stars burn...*
> *O, sea rover, fight...*

The storm split roofs and hurled boats ashore, uprooting trees, damaging walls.

Slowly, the old town pulls itself together.

Old town—you have seen many storms during your centuries. Is it true, you let this one slip past you and sent it to sea? You should have kept it! You can withstand battering better than a small ship! Is it true, what the fishermen say, that many were drowned?

Men and boys go about town, picking up tiles to load their baskets.

Driftwood clutters the beach.

Men were hurling stones, grabbing them off the beach and throwing them. I heard them hit Pittakos and saw him stagger, his flapping rags jerking, his arm flung over his eyes. Silent, feet wide apart, he stayed his ground.

Alcaeus, facing the sea, lidless-eyed, roared and lunged about, arms extended, yelling:

"Kill him...kill him...let me wring his neck!"

Beside him, the madman off the raft, howled and hurled stones.

About a dozen men were circling Pittakos, most of them blabbing defiance, closing in.

I rushed to Alcaeus and squeezed past him, to cry out... I told them to stop, asking them to stop in the name of our island, our town.

"Get back," Alcaeus warned.

I faced them, feeling their hate: it bubbled through me, seemed to ooze from the sand, from the sea, from antiquity: the hates of my ancestors, hatred of tyranny and unfairness.

No one threw: they watched me, as I walked toward Pittakos: maybe they thought I had a stone.

"You get back," I cried. "Go home, before they kill you, Pittakos. Get back everyone...go home."

Nervously folding and unfolding his robe, Pittakos backed away. A hand went to a spot where a stone must have struck. I felt no pity but stepped closer.

"I don't know what caused these men to turn on you... I don't want to know...go home, before it's too late."

Without replying, he shuffled away, a sandal off.

"Is he going?" asked Alcaeus, finding me, hand on my shoulder.

"Let him go," I said, facing the others.

Grasping Alcaeus, I forced him to walk with me, muttering to him, seeing Thasos, dropping his stones with a guilty grin.

I wanted to forget the faces but I knew most of the men: young, bearded faces, most of them friends of Alcaeus, some of them his soldiers.

"Don't lead me," Alcaeus protested.

"You need to be led."

"You came at the wrong time."

"What's to become of you?"

"Let me go," he said.

"I'll see you home. Here, Thasos, take his arm. Thasos, were you mad?"

"We should have stoned him."

"Why?"

"He quarreled with Alcaeus—spat on him."

Alcaeus leaned on me and I sensed his weariness as if it were mine: he was breathing hard and had to rest, stopping again and again. Behind us, his madman wandered, his Pamphilus.

"I'm too old for this kind of horseplay, it seems."

Thasos and I were saddened by his tragic features; we frowned; minute wrinkles had enlarged and deepened; his hands trembled; his mouth was open. He seemed in the past, with his men, galled, waiting: What is memory for, I asked myself, to crucify? Shut off from the day, is this the best memory can do?

When I sat with him at home, I said:

"What was the quarrel about?"

"First, some water."

Thasos brought us water. The cool of his gourd helped.

"Pittakos has stolen from the city...again...I came at him with the facts...I know the truth...many of us know."

We remained silent a while, my hand in his.

"It's an old truth—for us," I said.

"Very old," he said.

Presently, the madman entered, carrying himself stiffly, chalk faced, chastised.

Oblivious of us, appearing more normal than any time I had seen him, he talked with Thasos, regretting the incident.

Soft-talking men, inside an inner room, brought home to me the innocence of our own lives, how based on impulse, how like kelp, twisting, sinking, headed for shore, dragged to sea: we are mad, we are sane, or between: we exert ourselves and the world seeks revenge; we accept and earn ridicule and belittlement: we affirm ourselves and alter our lives and the lives of others: war is such an affirmation.

Innocence? Why not call all life innocent because dependability can not be assured. And, if life is innocent, then what is there but compassion and patience and kindness and beauty and love?

"It would have been better if they had killed him," Alcaeus said, rubbing his hands over his face.

I said nothing.

"I could have him murdered," he said.

"Alcaeus...wait..."

"Wait? How much longer must we wait?"

"He's old."

"Are we children?"

"He knows what's happening."

"No—not even yet."

"That couldn't be."

I saw Pittakos by the sea, spray dampening his clothes, his mouth to the gulls: I saw him, hand over eyes, legs spread; I heard stones hitting him... I could take no more and saying good-bye to Alcaeus, I walked home, eager to be alone, for now the town seemed withdrawn, callous, incomplete, a failure. I touched a hollow in a wall and picked a leaf and, where a street opened on the bay, looked and looked: the sea's salty taste acted as a philter and years of contentment and ease surged about me, trying to reinstate themselves: my girls met me and we went home together, sharing our innocence.

Just the other day, I dreamed of Serfo's place, his fabrics around me, things from Assyria, Egypt and Persia. Some of the cloth blew against me, light as a Sudanese veil. Atthis had a length of it in her hands, a twisted flowered piece yards long.

"I'll make ribbons for your hair," she said.

Alone, I sank into patterns, colors and textures. Something brushed my cheek, a winged bull in gold on blue cotton... I saw an imperial snake in green on white silk, a mighty roc in black on grey wool... I heard friends asking prices, Anaktoria, Libus.

I heard mother say:

"This is the best, this one, darling, with temples and shields on it, this blue, soft blue! Don't you love it? Here, take it in your hands, press it to your face."

I saw ships and listened to their keels...sailors unloading bales...wasn't that a remnant on the water?

A suffusion of light envelopes the Venus de Milo,
revealing the contours and texture of her hair,
face, breasts, belly, and drapery.
Voices sing Homeric hymns.
A woman, as lovely as the Milo,
disappears in the golden light
beneath the Mediterranean.

.

Was it three years ago I met Atthis—five years ago Anaktoria? Was that another dream? I am not sure.

Awake, I thought about my girls and now much they love me and make my house a house of grace. I must have beauty: I must have peace: and they are peace and beauty. I recalled how and when I had met each and loved each one for her special qualities. Each had a place in my heart, gold on cotton, green on white...the sea was at each meeting and at each good-bye... I count my years but the sea has no calendar.

Sometimes I feel the sea thinks for us, its pensiveness communicates at dawn, its meditation at night, its probity sifting through the day. A stormy emotion— the sea. A period of tranquility—the sea. Fickleness—the sea. I could not be happy without its communication. For all its pervasiveness it seems on the verge of a secret: looking down through the waves I sense it, I sense it at night, when phosphorescence steals shoreward or when rain obliterates and there is no visible ocean, then, still, still it communes, insinuating mystery, legends from caves, legends stronger than any coral, barracuda and stingrays roiled under, sinking farther and farther.

As we eat, in the dining room, Atthis prattles about her new parrot, mimicking it.

Her glances, charming, rounded, sensual, inconclusive, ask for love.

Her mimicry, spoken somewhat under her breath, takes in the townspeople, theatre folk, the Athenian star, Alcaeus, Gogu, the girls. But, because it is kindly and feminine, the fun carries far.

Her eyebrows have grown to meet over her nose and the fuzzy little bridge gives her added years. Her breasts are larger, shoulders fuller. She could be a priestess: the face solemn, the lips pert; then laughter ruins everything and she is simply girl, joyous life, asking for love.

Dressed in thin summer best, she pokes her neighbor with her sharp sandal and before I can say a word a scrap follows.

As I went downstairs, I put my hand between the lion's jaws, stubby, mossy stone, oldest part of the house. Lingering, I watched leaves puff down the steps. By the fountain, I absorbed water shadows, warmth around me, an insect swimming toward a spot of sun.

A village girl brought me a bouquet of white roses, saying:
"You must let me join your *hetaerae.*"
She wore a twisted blue wool skirt, of darkest color, and no blouse. Standing erect, she offered her flowers and then spun around and fled: I could scarcely take in the clean-cut features, pointed chin, red mouth and new breasts.
I can't imagine who she is or where she lives but I must find her.

My working hours are longer and as I review my work I find it good: that is a sign of maturity: maturity is the seal I strive for and yet as I work I fear a loss of spirit: maturity is seldom daring and to be daring is to open doors: maturity, then, is balance: is it also the decorum people accuse me of? Parasol, tilted at just the proper angle? Mask, worn at the right moments? As I came home yesterday from the play, I remembered a winking mask, rather like one in my room: was that derision?

I saw a young man on the street who startled me. Though he didn't glance at me, I thought I had seen him in Samnos: ax beard and sullen mouth were the same; he had the same slouch, the same filthy clothes. Watching him, I recalled that Samnian fellow, his pleas and questions:
"...tell nobody I'm here...but I want to know about home...tell me the news! You see I've been here for three years...to escape the war...there are three of us...we came here on a raft...tell us..."
The frenzied talk was vivid as this derelict walked down our street.
In Samnos, I had sympathized with my countryman for his voluntary exile was no easier than an enforced exile: I drew him out and later met his friends, all

hungry for news, all in rags, living from hand to mouth, scared. It was their fear that worried me and I urged them to make friends and forget the past, to marry and begin life in Samnos. I arranged contacts for them...

But, was this one of them sneaking along, hoping for luck? Pittakos, the wise, the clement, would have him lashed to death by nightfall, if someone discovered him. My pledge of secrecy is a pledge I'll keep. As I sailed home from Samnos, I thought of these men and was proud of their folly.

Roses are in bloom on the hills and violets are in flower around my house. Kleis will be married soon, so I am doing things wrong. I try to tell myself this is her happiest time and struggle to write a poem for her wedding. Her natural gaiety is infectious and yet, and yet...

We will have quite a ceremony, Libus, Alcaeus, Gogu, Nanno, Helen, my girls, sailors, half the town, Pittakos and rogues...Rhodopis and Charaxos...no, harshness is not in keeping with a wedding.

I can hear the male chorus.

I hear the surf...

Below us, the ocean eats at its rocks, above us lie the hills, around us stir the branches of the olives.

Peace: sacred grove, we dedicate these two: give them luck: a light will fall: the chorus will resume: a wreath will be hung.

Shall I play my harp?

Who is the god of illusion? Love? How is he to be kept alive through many years and many disappointments?

I shall try to help. Song has that gift, a gift nothing else has: to give the lost or hold it in suspension.

I feel utterly ridiculous, the greatest hypocrite: that is how it seems as I urge Alcaeus to curb his resentment for Pittakos.

I have tried reason but it isn't reason that moves Alcaeus. When he feels my sympathy, he listens: if he conceives of us as he used to be, his hatred subsides. Let him feel alone, he thunders, bends toward me, drags his fingers through his beard and sputters:

"To hear you talk, I'd think you were never mistreated by this man!"

"But you know better."

"You're a traitor to yourself!"

"That's not true. You want to have him killed and I say we lose through violence. I'm no traitor to myself—or you. You can be traitor to justice."

"Let's not say anything about justice, when we're fighting tyranny."

I recalled days with Aesop and said:

"I wish he was here, to advise us or hear our problems. I think I know what he'd say."

"What?"

"There's a way out of slavery... I didn't kill my master."

Slavery—there are all kinds.

It is a kind of slavery to long for Phaon and another kind to remember Aesop and another to hope. Perhaps Aesop would rebuke such thinking and say: Slavery is not in ourselves but in the misused power of others. Surely that is the commoner kind but I find slavery in myself and my girls and my island and my books.

Well, here is a story Phaon told me:

"Years ago, a slave broke into a temple on a deserted island and found lamps burning. On a rug lay a naked man, asleep. He'd been lying there for centuries, guarded by someone, the lamps filled and the wicks new.

"The King of Freedom, were the words on a shield beside him. His yellow hair streamed across the rug. Above him, a mask, fastened on the wall, spoke:

"'Shut the temple...let the lamps burn...make no noise...take a hair from his head...go.'

"The slave shut the temple, carefully.

"Years later, in prison, he bent over to examine the golden hair he had kept and it burst into flame and became a torch which he used to light his way to freedom."

His flames and heat are fuel
For seaman's muscles, his sea eyes,

Devil of laughter and devil moods,
His sinking-rising delicacy.

The initial union is relief
Of olives and cypress, breasts, birds,
Stinging and perspiration's siege,
Roots climbing out of centuries.

Beauty, the wedding is over and I am alone with my lighted lamps and moonlight across the sea, night's indifference.

Beauty, Kleis was happy...many of us were happy.

After the ceremony, Pittakos approached me, shuffling, dressed as I had never seen him dressed, in fine white clothes. His hate was gone, that was something I saw at once: I was seeing another man. Speaking guardedly, hands folding and unfolding his robe, he said:

"...They would have stoned me. What can I say...to make amends? You stopped them from killing me... You...you helped me..."

I grew confused. Remembering Alcaeus' threat, my hatred surged and I thought: Can he expect me to rub out the past because of an accident on my part? Can he ask such a thing?

Do you think that I have changed—that I went out of my way to save you?

My own harshness pained me. I had seen him at a distance, during the ceremony, and had resented his presence; as I played my harp and sang he remained near, boggling his head.

Our sacred grove, filled with people, trees streaked with fog, was still in my mind. I could see Kleis smiling and hear the wedding chorus, the flutists, the barking dogs, the cries of gulls.

Glancing overhead, I noticed them, passing, gliding, saying with their grace things I tried to say in my writing.

Pittakos turned away.

I could not say a word but stepped forward.

"...Pittakos."

He regarded me doubtfully.

"Yes."

Then I started to walk away.

"What can I say? I'm old... I can't erase errors. Sappho, I... Last night I stayed up all night...it was more than thinking: I looked at the past. I've been mistaken. Though we've lived here, in this town, we know only lies about each other..."

Shuffling, he made off.

All were there in the grove: Alcaeus, baffled; Libus, pale and aloof; Anaktoria, gay; Atthis, dreaming; Kleis, my herder... We ate together, drank, sang... The sun drank the fog and sunset ribboned the ocean.

I shall remember goats wandering through our grove, tinkling their bells...the mask-maker carrying my harp for me...trying to sing in toothless ecstasy...I shall remember the altar fire and wreaths of flowers, their incense and coloring... remember, too, the farewell of my pair, their backs and shoulders as they headed for their house on the headland, a small place among figs and tall white poppies, their world—not mine. I must remember it is their world. When Kleis flings her arms around me I will rejoice. At the same time, I must accept the fact that their marriage is their particular freedom.

May it be a satisfying freedom.

Mother's lamp, as I write, is nearly empty: she would have liked the wedding ceremony, the chorus singing my poem: terra-cotta lamp, do you remember her wedding? Did you burn for her ecstasy or were you snuffed out before the groom carried her to bed?

It wasn't long ago I was married: how I walked, my head high, the embodiment of innocence and grace: I thought life would be easy!

The wind puffs through my room.

The ocean whispers.

Charaxos and Rhodopis attended the wedding, staying apart with a group of their friends, no one dressed for the occasion. Since the man who had forcibly made love to her was there, I was disconcerted. I was ashamed. My face burned. What could I do? Would they interfere? But they seemed preoccupied, merely onlookers, most of them young men and women.

When they sauntered away, I enjoyed the wedding.

Someone among them, a stranger perhaps, gazed back at me, reminding me of Cercolas.

Cercolas, my mother, Aesop—each summons a series of images. When each one died, I thought: How can I go on? Now my thought is: What has replaced them? Husband, mother, friend... I am forever altered by their absence, emptier, lonelier. I seek them in others and yet never find them.

It matters to me how they died.

I am still troubled that Cercolas died on the battlefield. And it is tragic that Aesop died, beaten by a mob. At least, mother died beside me, comforted as much as human comfort is possible.

Death should not catch us unaware for then it cheats us doubly. Surely, it is hard enough to die without dying in some tragic way. Each of us deserves a last dignity.

Shall I tell Alcaeus that Pittakos came to me after the wedding?

I may never tell him because he will suffer more for knowing. It seems to me telling him could accomplish little. Hard as it is, unfair as it is, I must keep this to myself. Of course, some would disbelieve. And if Pittakos sees fit to remain silent, he and I will be better off. Lives will be less complicated.

Even unmolested, he has not much time ahead. We must be far-sighted and choose a leader...

Homosexual lovers in bed,
making love in the moonlight.
The light falls on their flesh,
faces, hands, legs, their passion:
laughter and soft moans and
the ocean below the villa.
Sappho rises and ponders her body,
stands by a window, facing the Aegean.

I took my lyre and said:
Here, now, my heavenly
Tortoise shell, become
A speaking instrument.

One by one, the poems have fitted into my book, so slowly time seems to have had nothing to do with its completion. Yet, my ninth book is done. When I had finished my sixth, I thought: this is all. When I finished my eighth, I felt I need go no farther. Will there be a tenth? What will make it distinctive?

Phaon lives in this book, insatiability floods everywhere: lyric by lyric, our smoldering hearts reveal our happiness.

When I shared lines with him, he laughed at their frankness, eyes dancing. He remembered some of them, and shot them back at me, to tease.

I have sent selections to Solon: what will he write me? Will their crudeness be too much for him? I think not. He has savored love.

My Egyptians are copying the book—conspirators, no doubt, mumbling lines to each other, shaking heads. I'd like to slip into their shop as they work, to overhear them: would I laugh or recoil? Probably I'd be annoyed. Well, tomorrow I must go to the shop and see how they are doing.

I have not thought of a title.

Villa Poseidon

I sought Anaktoria and together we spent the night.

In spite of her comfort, I could not get to sleep. Her arms around me, she lay motionless.

During the afternoon, we arranged flowers, taking them from the garden. A rainbow appeared over the bay and arm in arm we watched it, its arc faintly reflected on the water. Her myrrh was everywhere, her spirit too: the things she said were right: family traditions are a part of her and she adds just enough fantasy.

For a while, we practiced archery, her shooting more accurate than mine. A lost arrow sent us near the sea. Then games...games...what would life be without games and laughter!

Watch the dice in her fingers!

She's a magician of tricks and youth, my Anaktoria and, oddly enough, I can never bring it all together; it is too effervescent, too delightful: the moment swells over us: then, another moment, even while we are eating together, growing sleepy together: ours is a gift that has come from our island without men, years of femininity.

Someone sent me the doll Aesop had when he died, his Cretan doll. It came from Adelphi; badly wrapped, I opened it in my library, laid it on my desk, amazed to see it, startled, fingers fumbling. Someone had wanted to be kind, but it wasn't kindness to send it. What faded colors, what worn cloth, how had the doll gotten this old? It had suffered another kind of death.

With the doll in my arms, I smelled the incense of his house, dinner on the table, fresh fruit piled before us: the broad bracelet he wore bothered him and he shoved it higher on his arm: silent tonight, he listened to what we had been doing during the day: he had such heart for Alcaeus and me.

I could not keep the figure but packed it away. Its evocative intimacy, its forlorn quality...they would serve no purpose I could think of. I was glad Alcaeus could not see it. Yet, I felt I had rejected Aesop.

A sweltering day was made worse when Gogu had a seizure near Serfo's shop. Serfo and Libus carried him inside and I found them working over Gogu, kneeling beside him, Serfo's slave fanning the sick man, swaying his palm frond low, Libus' face tense and canvas-colored. Serfo turned his barbaric features, square-cut beard and blazing green eyes, on me, resentful when I placed a damp sponge on Gogu's head, when I suggested we pull him farther away from the wall. He growled and backed off, to care for some customers.

"Is it Gogu's old trouble?" I asked.

Libus nodded, his hands comforting the man. When Gogu's teeth chattered and his head and shoulders shook, Libus restrained him, hands on his shoulders. When he spoke to Gogu, I could detect an immediate response. The slave brought water and poured it for Gogu and Libus got him to drink: the frond dipping closer, rising and falling. "Libus—Libus," he said, and sighed, thin lashes over upturned eyes. The black hitched his broadcloth and sighed too.

The room was windowless and cool, lit from overhead. A pigeon cooed on the roof. For a while I sat near Libus but when Serfo offered drinks, we went into his shop where he displayed ivory figurines on his dusty counter, Amazons, ibis, Etruscan warriors and sacred cats, none bigger than my hand.

"The cats are from Luxor," Serfo said.

"Will Gogu be all right?" I asked, hearing his rapid breathing.

"He'll be all right by evening," Libus said.

So we examined the collection, Libus questioning their antiquity: I pointed out the yellowing and flaking: he held an Amazon in the doorway, dust cracks mottling her face and armor, the texture of his hands obvious as well.

He seems to be holding me in his fingers, as small. I felt the flakes of time— my life flaking, like Gogu's, less lasting than the ivory.

The hours I spend with Libus and his sister are hours of talk and wine, at his small house, in its garden of figs and olives, poppies in bloom along the paths. Their place, nearer the bay than mine, absorbs the bay's placidity. The furniture stresses comfort. His mosaics reflect his regard for ease...scenes of old days and old creatures.

I was glad when Libus gave up staying with Alcaeus; I had missed those visits to his home where Helen has taught me designs for my loom and reaffirmed what patience really is. She has read to me, acquainting me with books I would never have found...

Libus talks and toys with a loop of beads, in a thoughtful mood, his hands, as they move, remind me of their healing quality and his voice has that same beneficence, distinctly personal, meanings having extra meaning most of the time.

Helen's face has none of his ephemerality but has, instead, a country wholesomeness I love. She chats about flowers she has grown, seeds she keeps in jars, promising me a selection.

Their poppies, grey-leafed, sea-bitten, have large centers and bees loll on the petals and the sea lolls beyond them.

Why is it the hours loll here? I have seen whales from their garden, sporting near beds of kelp, their blue backs like so many watery hills. I think something lures them offshore...another something makes Libus' servants sing more than my servants.

A gigantic sea-rock assumes the face of a crying woman when the fog comes: some say she cries for our dead in the wars, some say it's for those lost at sea: I have often seen her, head bowed: she faces the town, staring: the sea sound is her weeping; perhaps it is the weeping of many women: if I walk by that deserted spot at night, with the fog about me, I cling to Atthis or Exekias. No woman goes alone there, when the fog is about.

The moon has set and
The Pleiades have gone;
The night is half gone
And life speeds by.
I lie in bed, alone.

Going to see Alcaeus, I met Kleis and she threw her arms around me and kissed me, saying:

"Mama, dear, it's good to see you! How I miss you!"

I tried to hide my pleasure but my heart sang and I held her close, my body remembering hers, fingers slipping around the back of her neck, staying in her hair.

Pushing me aside, she exclaimed:

"Mama, let's go to your house and be together, like old times. Shall we?"

How easy to consent—and we walked home, arms around each other, gulls over us, shadows skimming roofs, dusty cobbles asking for rain: I wanted to remember her chatter, each inflection...

I would see Alcaeus tomorrow. I needed time with my own...

Pittakos stoned...Aesop stoned...the mob's disgrace...

Year after year, is there greater calumny than our own communal perfidy? Is there greater stupidity? One man starts it, then five, then ten, manacled together.

For our island's sake, I'm glad I cheated death.

Like old times, we sat at our looms and Kleis showed me a periwinkle design, whispering confidences, saying he was good, saying the house was good, the sea...she put her faith on the loom, the thread of it going beyond life. Mother must have heard me say such things, reflecting the same hope. Finches gathered in the olive trees as we worked. I asked time to stop and let us have the day last, at least longer than evening and the shepherd's bells.

Charaxos brought him to my house, a castaway, I thought, dreg of the worst sea. Charaxos stood behind him in Cairo red, the sun blazing over the town, as the castaway bowed, holding together his rags, eyes wandering, skin and bones, nose snuffing at his hand, his mouth lower on one side, a canine look on his face.

Muttering, he fished in a sack tied about his waist and offered me something.

I hesitated to take it, feeling Charaxos' curiosity—or was it gloating? I grew afraid as the castaway insisted, wagging head and hand, Charaxos silent; forcing myself, I bent and peered at his hand...seeing a drachma.

I saw it had been pierced for a chain...taking it, I made out the letters my mother had gouged...in the metal...yes, it was her drachma.

I wanted to run, throw down the coin, send Charaxos away, turn aside the castaway. I wanted to crumble on the steps and bury my head in my arms and deny existence.

"Come in," I managed.

And the men entered.

Together, we sat down and I asked:

"Where did you get the coin?"

"At Cos..."

"You are from Cos?"

"Yes, I came from Cos."

"He came on one of my ships," Charaxos said.

I could not look at either man.

"He came from Cos," I said.

"Phaon died on the island...he and others...thrown on the beach...we have rocky shores...he was injured in the big storm...you see, we found him, my wife and son and I. He gave us the coin and sent me to you...he..."

So, he died after that storm, I told myself, and I got up, wondering where I could go: I saw the castaway's blazing eyes and torn clothing and the greedy face of my brother:

"Stay at my house...as long as you like," I said. "I will send servants to look after you. I will..."

What will I do? I asked myself.

Will I take the coin and sleep with it? Will it burn my bed? Will I place it on my desk or hurl it out my window? And I opened my fingers to see if the bronze was on fire.

Now, you have seen me grief-stricken, I thought, as I gazed at Charaxos. You may go and tell your friends. Tell them, Sappho is beaten. Tell them...

I excused myself and retreated to my room.

Far at sea, I saw a dot: Phaon's ship, and I opened my hand and laid his drachma on the windowsill.

Beauty, is he dead?

What has been gained by taking him from me?

Shall I go to Xerxes, and hold him to his promise? Couldn't there be a mistake? Better to find Xerxes and say to him, "Remember your promise," and take his powder. This is my inheritance, from parents, Cercolas, friends, this degree of misfortune, final degradation. Was love a mirage, or this?

Libus sat beside my bed, his hands alleviating the pain that dragged at every nerve: his hands warmed me, crossing my back and shoulders, assuaging with their mirage the storm that seemed everywhere inside me, bursting my throat, my brain, my chest, shattering my reason.

Yet, as he helped me, he reasoned:

"I hoped he would be back early enough for Kleis' wedding...he said something to me about getting back early... I hoped you two would go on...you know all of us watched you...our hearts were yours...it was like that.

"I've always thought your pride deserved love, Phaon's kind, free of politics. Yes, I know Alcaeus was sufficient, years ago; then our island women adopted you; then Phaon. It was his luck to give you what you needed..."

"My coin didn't bring luck to him," I said.

"A coin means what? Metal can't tell us about life...only we can tell...to one another..."

"What have I told you through the years?"

He paused a while, hands motionless.

"Beauty..."

"And now?"

"Another kind...in the making. I know your ancestral line...losses become gain...I recognize bravery."

His hands and thoughts continued their palliative, now the fingers, now the voice, as servants replaced lamps and closed windows, moving as slowly as if below the sea, finally to leave us alone again, the ocean's voice mixing with the crickets.

"Kleis will bring Phaon back to me," I said.

"Theirs is a curious resemblance...I agree."

"What will happen to his house?"

"It will be hers," he said.

"But she'll never live in town."

"No...she won't change her ways."

"Have you ever liked his house? I haven't."

"No," he said.

"Libus, why doesn't Alcaeus come to me?"

"He's not thinking of your problem."

"He doesn't know about Phaon?"

"He knows...but can't come."

"Shall I go to him?"

"Wait...for a while," he said.

My girls seldom leave me: Atthis, Gyrinno, Anaktoria, each brings flowers and gifts, bringing them surreptitiously or with a hint of jollity—sometimes compassion. Old Exekias pats my hands, kisses my skirt or turns away, tears unchecked.

Atthis, cheek against mine, murmurs her love. As we walk through our garden she says:

"I miss him too... I loved him too... We placed a wreath for him... We three have made a shrine in the woods..."

Gyrinno appears in the night, as I lie sleepless. Unable to mention the tragedy, she whispers hoarsely that she loves me and wants to help: Is there anything she can do for me?

Anaktoria has probed deeper:

"You must take care, Sappho. You must do nothing strange, that would harm us. We can't have you obsessed by melancholy. Let us look after you."

Eyes streaked with tears dim and I see him, imagine his body sprawled between the rocks of Cos and I hear his voice speak my name: I see our Leucadian cliff and know I could throw myself down, die as he died among the rocks, far below.

Then, I find Kleis as I work at my loom, and her voice, revealing her sorrow, eradicates the drama of self: the curse of death needs soft hands and blonde hair and blue eyes and tender mouth... "Mama, darling..."

Sometimes I try to brush aside feminine ties, but there they are, tightening about me: snatches of song come to me: I see women with babies at the fountain; vineyards creep over the hills, ascending through fog, under the wings of gulls, moving toward me, closer and closer: they are my father's vineyards, the vineyards of Alcaeus, Phaon's vineyards, Libus', Anaktoria's; the bone flute, the whole island is in them, in the spring leaves and autumn leaves, in the stark vines of winter: the weeping rock moves through them, the defeated fleet, the red rooftops of home, the bare hills, olive trees: I see a woman, called Sappho, leading a child, named Kleis: I hear shepherd's bells, and the silence of dawn spills up from the ocean's shore: a porpoise and a whale, beyond a belt of kelp, churn points of light and shadow: home, home is the red tiles and my mother's lamps and the view where the vineyards snuggle to sleep for the night: this is my inheritance, to keep as long as possible, that is what I tell myself, compel myself to feel.

Kleis has the grape leaf woven in her loom and as she weaves she faces me and smiles and I know how much love is in that smile.

Sappho stands by the seaward window in her library...
carved ivory racks hold books, ancient papyri,
Egyptian clay tablets, copies of hymns.
Blue from the bay inundates the library, her face,
obliterates the books.
Alcaeus, an old man,
holds a tattered manuscript.

S uddenly, he stood in front of me, in my library, dressed in black, beard soiled, deep wrinkles underneath his eyes.

"Alcaeus, I didn't hear you and Thasos."

"Exekias let us in. Are you working?"

"No...sit down."

"Are you alone?"

"Yes."

He leaned on Thasos: I felt that he hadn't been sober very long; he leaned forward, almost stumbling.

"Can I sit down?"

"Here, here," said Thasos, helping him, laying aside a package.

Silence troubled us.

I watched Thasos go and then Alcaeus said:

"I understand your loss. I understand what has happened to you. Phaon's death has overpowered you. I put it badly...but we have shared...be patient...I understand...Sappho; I have brought you my Homer. Remember, when I got it years ago? Remember? I want to share. I should have given you this before...What good is it to me?"

"Alcaeus."

"Where is the book?"

"The package Thasos left?"

"Yes...take it...open it..."

I opened it, remembering how we had thrilled long ago, and, after a while, reaching out to him, grateful, hoping I could make him sense my gratitude, I kissed his forehead and his hands, his hands motionless, the sightless eyes confusing me.

He went on slowly:

"I've come to share my strength...it's a poor strength, drunk, blind, but it does go on. You, my dear, are blinded by grief. Let me tell you your grief can't be as bad as mine. Or, if it is, let's share...share...we've shared before...I'll take your dark away...hide it in mine...lose some of your burden at least.

"Sappho, let me help.

"Accept the old book, find hope in it... I have kicked aside death on the field...look at my eyes and then look at yours...you need no mirror.

"He's dead...dead by the sea...you have your love of beauty to uphold you.

Let it live! Give it new life! Soon enough death will claim both of us, but, till then, let's find comradeship...come to my house tomorrow, read to me...

"Will you?"

I nodded, then remembered he could not see and remembered his gift and his grace and knelt by him and put my head in his hands and pressed between his knees, as he patted me, chuckling a little.

"I'll come tomorrow, Alcaeus," I promised.

"Good."

"I know your lot is worse than mine... I must find courage."

Beauty, I thought, beauty, what can I say to help this man?

"Yes, tomorrow; then I'll tell you, Sappho... I'll tell you what I've learned, living in my black sea. How my ship drags anchor. What I've heard. I've heard some strange things. I can sense someone moving, almost before he moves, a shift of air, let's say.

"Watch me play jacks with Libus, old soldiers at their fun. I could cheat you...if you gave me half a chance."

Again that chuckle.

The book lay open and his great arms lay across his lap, fingers up. My father had owned that book. With age it had come unsewed and hung in tatters: the smell of age was there: I rubbed my fingers over pages...

Quickly, he said:

"I like to feel those pages... I wanted to write a book as full of life...give back the thunder of the storm...look how the bugs have eaten the book...see that ripped page...well, where will you keep your Homer?"

And he smiled.

"Shall I read something?"

"Yes...now!"

Turning the pages so he could hear them I searched for a favorite passage.

I read as slowly and as distinctly as possible, allowing each word time.

Cercolas, mother, Aesop, Phaon...gone. When shall I go?

I have been unable to write for days. I have nothing to say...there is only emptiness.

Yesterday a nightingale sang, a song of tattered leaves, scraps of Nile, bits of Euphrates, papyrus against night, against impending doom, against depression. Tender notes whispered insanity. Other notes urged self-pity. Others shattered—with sheerest delicacy—any hope of contrition.

A feather drops...a pause. One could die during such a pause.

All of us wait—life waits!

A bubbling deceives the spirit, a trill alienates the heart. Something summons the past, other songs on other nights, other songs of other people, the bone flute, of course.

This was not a bird, not a beak, not a feather but sail and spar, rigged to go at dawn, course along many shores.

"Beauty, you're frail. Your bones are able to carry next to nothing and yet your song travels, spreading as if a pebble had dropped on water..."

I walked under olive trees along the coast, following grassy paths, the breeze with me until I met Gogu, carrying a piece of kelp and a shell. At first, he did not seem to recognize me. How thin, how sick he is! Shadows of the olives shadowed him. When he spoke, I hardly listened. Each of us is going the same way, I thought, and so we parted and stillness put its loneliness about me. The words he had said mixed me because I had not listened, mixed with my love-memories, adding incoherence.

Why was Gogu carrying kelp and a shell? Why was I walking where I had often walked?

In a hundred years, this path has changed little: the trees have become more gnarled, the shadows darker, the air quieter.

The marble shrine at the end of the path crumbles year by year and yet remains about the same: I can remember it when another brought me: Phaon remembered it: and now, memories are re-dedicated and burned, their ashes under my sandals, under my fingers and heart.

The best of life is illusion, I do not doubt. The best of Phaon may have been illusion.

Ah, the nettles of desire, the sleeplessness, the gnawing of regrets in my skull. These are emotions we can not share but must suffer alone till dawn, the dipper proving we are children.

I believe that we, as human beings, prove nothing: there is really nothing to prove except kindness and decency: all else is more illusion.

I take my harp but there are no words to accompany the notes. I urge Atthis to sing: play, darling, help me forget...let me see your face as I love to see it. Move your head with that fragile alacrity. Stretch your bare legs under your dress.

As I open the shutters in the morning, I miss him...the ocean has grown much, much wider.

My favorite olive tree says nothing to me.

Alcaeus wrote me:

"I know I can help you. Come over for the day. Courage, friend."

The note repulsed me. What could he know of Phaon, of man's cleanliness and beauty!

I did not answer. Instead, I climbed the hills with Atthis and Anaktoria, to lay a wreath at an altar that has been our shrine for a while.

The sea was rough and the wind was rough.

Tears overcame me at the altar and I made them leave me: I hoped to die there: I wanted my bitterness to kill me: Why couldn't it happen? Why couldn't there be this finality?

I pulled flowers from the wreath and wrote his name on the ground. A thrush hopped close by. The wind, gusting from the bay, scattered blossoms and I found Atthis beside me, kneeling to comfort me. We had shared so much, the three of us, days and weeks, grief and joy. She and Anaktoria got me to eat, under pines sheltered from the wind; she and Anaktoria fixed my hair.

Their sad faces made me long for happiness for their sake, and I tried to see beyond myself. There must be a trick that I can use to deceive others.

The placid sea carries a few boats,
small clouds on the horizon,
a series of silver cat's-paws;
and as though through a sheet
of green glass the faces of
Sappho, Atthis and Anaktoria:
a laurel wreath whirls above the Aegean:
herons fly, dolphins leap.

K leis left her shepherd's hut and came here and we have talked far into the night:

"He liked a gold cup...he liked the mountains...he liked the cove...yes, he went farther out to sea than anyone...his sailors liked him...he..."

Kleis stayed several days and each day was a mirror of his personality. Her beauty brought out his quality, imaging it in various ways, her nature shaken from its customary silence to talk of him. I recognized the effort and appreciated the communication. I wanted to write her notes but she could not read. I wanted to thank her in some special way but it was she who thanked me, before slipping away.

Afterward I counted other friends: Alcaeus, Libus, Helen, Exekias, Atthis, Anaktoria, Gyrinno, Heptha, Gogu... I also counted those who have died. Dreaming, I counted our island, our town, our trees, mountains and sea. I added my home. However childish to enumerate like this, I went to sleep easily.

Perhaps, as I grow older, I may find an idea, a seed. Perhaps it can grow in someone's mind: compassion, courage, grace, love—it could become one of these.

I shall continue to put down my thoughts, the handprint of my days.

Could it be that the greatest thing in life is perseverance?

Somebody, I tell you,
Someone in future time
Will remember us.

We are oppressed by
oblivion, by the idea
Of nothing at all,

Yet are saved by the
Judgment of good men.

ABOUT THE AUTHOR

*P*aul Alexander Bartlett (1909-1990) was a writer and artist, born in Moberly, Missouri, and educated at Oberlin College, the University of Arizona, the Academia de San Carlos in Mexico City, and the Instituto de Bellas Artes in Guadalajara. His work can be divided into three categories: He is the author of many novels, short stories, and poems; second, as a fine artist, his drawings, illustrations, and paintings have been exhibited in more than forty one-man shows in leading galleries, including the Los Angeles County Museum, the Atlanta Art Museum, the Bancroft Library, the Richmond Art Institute, the Brooks Museum, the Instituto-Mexicano-Norteamericano in Mexico City, and many other galleries; and, third, he devoted much of his life to the most comprehensive study of the haciendas of Mexico that has been undertaken. More than 350 of his pen-and-ink illustrations of the

haciendas and more than one thousand hacienda photographs make up the Paul Alexander Bartlett Collection held by the Nettie Lee Benson Latin American Collection of the University of Texas, and form part of a second diversified collection held by the American Heritage Center of the University of Wyoming, which also includes an archive of Bartlett's literary work, fine art, and letters.

Paul Alexander Bartlett's fiction has been commended by many authors, among them Pearl Buck, Ford Madox Ford, John Dos Passos, James Michener, Upton Sinclair, Evelyn Eaton, and many others. He was the recipient of many grants, awards, and fellowships, from such organizations as the Leopold Schepp Foundation, the Edward MacDowell Association, the New School for Social Research, the Huntington Hartford Foundation, the Montalvo Foundation, and the Carnegie Foundation.

His wife, Elizabeth Bartlett, a widely published poet, is the author of seventeen published books of poetry, numerous poems, short stories, and essays published in leading literary quarterlies and anthologies, and, as the founder of Literary Olympics, Inc., is the editor of a series of multi-language volumes of international poetry that honor the work of outstanding contemporary poets.

Paul and Elizabeth's son, Steven, edited and designed this volume.

Sappho's Journal

was set in Garamond type by Autograph Editions. The typeface is named after Claude Garamond (c. 1480-1561), a French type designer and publisher and the world's first commercial typefounder. Garamond's contribution to the history of typesetting was substantial. He perfected the design of Roman type: The fonts that he cut beginning in 1531 were recognized as possessing a superior grace and clarity, so much so that Garamond's fonts influenced European printing for the next century and a half.

It is interesting to note that Garamond type is the evolutionary ancestor of the type used to print the first official copies of the Declaration of Independence. In the 1730s, Englishman William Caslon refined Garamond's version of Aldine roman, the well-balanced typeface became popular, and was introduced to the American colonies by Benjamin Franklin.

Despite his considerable contribution to the evolution of typography, Garamond was not a successful businessman and he died in poverty.

During the past five centuries, so many variations of Garamond's type designs have been created that the phrase 'Garamond type' has come to be used loosely, with little memory remaining of its history.

www.ingramcontent.com/pod-product-compliance
Lightning Source LLC
Chambersburg PA
CBHW052136170626
46812CB00004B/1440